THE HOUSTILIAD

AN *ILIAD* FOR HOUSTON

BOOKS BY MICHAEL LIEBERMAN

POETRY
Praising with My Body
A History of the Sweetness of the World
Sojourn at Elmhurst
Remnant
Far-From-Equilibrium Conditions
Bonfire of the Verities
The Houstiliad

FICTION
Never Surrender—Never Retreat
The Lobsterman's Daughter
The Woman of Harvard Square

THE HOUSTILIAD

AN *ILIAD* FOR HOUSTON

MICHAEL LIEBERMAN

TEXAS REVIEW PRESS
HUNTSVILLE, TEXAS

FIRST EDITION

Requests for permission to acknowledge material from this work should be sent to:

Permissions
Texas Review Press
English Department
Sam Houston State University
Huntsville, TX 77341-2146

The Houstiliad is a work of fiction. All characters, locations, events, and incidents are products of the author's imagination or are used fictionally. Any resemblance to actual people, living or dead, or events is entirely coincidental.

To learn more about Michael Lieberman and his work or to contact him:

website: michaellieberman.com
email: poet@lieberman.net

Cover Design by Nancy Parsons

Library of Congress Cataloging-in-Publication Data

Lieberman, Michael, 1941- author.

The Houstiliad : an Iliad for Houston / Michael Lieberman. -- Edition: first.

pages cm

Summary: "In this nervy adaptation of Homer's classic, the story of Achilles' rage is told with a deft touch and a large dollop of humor. Achilles, an MIT-trained engineer, has dropped out and with Patroclus, his white macaw, cruises around Houston on an old BMW motorcycle looking for trouble. And he finds plenty. Along the way we meet Hector, the Hammer; Agamemnon, a wealthy Houston businessman with an eye for Achilles' girlfriend; Aphrodite, a custom bra designer; Apollo, owner of Café Apollo; and many of Homer's other characters, as Lieberman liberates them from their classical context. The result is a wry take on Houston and an uncompromising exploration of the rage of men in contemporary society"--ECIP Summary.

ISBN 978-1-68003-055-6 (pbk. : alk. paper)

1. Achilles (Mythological character)--Poetry. 2. Agamemnon, King of Mycenae (Mythological character)--Poetry. 3. Aphrodite (Greek deity)--Poetry. 4. Man-woman relationships--Texas--Houston--Poetry. 5. Fighting (Psychology)--Texas--Houston--Poetry. 6. Houston (Tex.)--Poetry. 7. Homer--Parodies, imitations, etc. I. Homer. Iliad. Adaptation of (work): II. Title.

PS3562.I434H68 2015

811'.54--dc23

2015018372

In memory of my father
For my sons Jonathan and Seth
and
my grandsons Casey, Julian, and Zachary

A gobsmacked doff to Pope and Homer—
one set the arrow's vector,
the other was its fletcher.

CONTENTS

INTRODUCTION

To attempt a book-length poem is surely a fool's errand in an age addicted to tweets and Instagram, one in which a photo or fifty words—a hundred tops—must convey the message. And all the more foolish if the poem is set in Houston, widely regarded as one of our country's less interesting or appealing cities. Can any poem that portrays the rage of men in modern society go head to head with the fast-paced thrillers of Jo Nesbo or Olen Steinhauer, the churning treachery of *Scandal* or *House of Cards*, the stark, lurid realism of *The Wire*? Even Superman seems lame: Today everything is faster than a speeding bullet. The world is too much with us.

Yet it always has been. Nineteen-hundred years before Wordsworth, Virgil's *Aeneid* had to compete with the racy lyrics of Catullus, not to mention the gladiators.

What has become *The Houstiliad, An* Iliad *for Houston* started as a short prose sketch, about 450 words, an intrusion that showed up uninvited one morning. It got its teeth into me and wouldn't let go. It took over my imagination, morphed, and accreted material from my reading, my thoughts, my experiences, and my day-to-day life in a neighborhood at the edge of the Montrose section of Houston. It then surprised me by becoming a long poem.

To tell this story I have appropriated characters from Homer's *Iliad*, reimagined and repurposed them, and set them in conflict in twenty-first century Houston. In *The Houstiliad*, Achilles, the hero of the Trojan War, appears as an MIT-trained engineer from a well-to-do Houston family who has dropped out and cruises around town on an old BMW motorcycle with a sidecar—he retains what Homer called "the wrath of Achilles." His rival Hector is an ex-marine and scion of a powerful, wealthy Latino family, the Martillos, hence the moniker, Hector the Hammer. The famous Helen of Troy appears as a young, wealthy matron from River Oaks, the most exclusive neighborhood in Houston. And Patroclus, Achilles' closest friend and second in *The Iliad*, has been transfigured to a white macaw who remains his constant companion. These and other characters, while uprooted to a present-day Houston, retain awareness of their ancestral origins. Certainly it's an odd, but necessary kind of self-knowledge.

Only poetry seemed capacious enough to encompass the theme and elastic enough to allow for its narrative flow. Taking a cue from Alexander Pope's unrivaled translation of *The Iliad*, I have provided a prose summary at the beginning of each book.

The actions of Homer's characters depend greatly on Fate and the whims of the gods. I have allowed them to intervene in this modern story as well. Why? Because they surely do, and their intercessions are often meddlesome and capricious. To breathe life into the gods, I have followed the lead of C.G. Jung and Joseph Campbell; their influence is everywhere in this story. And with the gods have come our shadows—our dark, largely unglimpsed, unseemly sides—and whimsy and humor as well.

In telling Houston's story and depicting the rage of men who live here, I have tried to preserve Homer's unflinching, graphic descriptions of violence and wrath, the tenderness of his portrayals of loves and friendships, his eclectic word choice, his love of lists, his use of epithets, and the quick pace of his verse.

I wrote largely without intent giving my unconscious free reign and unsure at times what story I was telling. It was only in looking back that I realized that by beginning with Homer and the rage of Achilles, my unconscious selected my subject—the rage of men in modern society. And while the setting is Houston, the city I know best, the events of *The Houstiliad* could have occurred almost anywhere in America.

CHARACTERS

ACHILLES AND HIS FRIENDS AND ALLIES

Achilles Peleuson, an MIT-trained engineer, who has dropped out, lives in Montrose—Houston's most eclectic neighborhood—and drives an old BMW motorcycle with a sidecar.

Patroclus, Achilles' white macaw and constant companion.

Briseis Priestly, Achilles' girlfriend, a University of Texas honors graduate, and waitress in a girly bar.

Agamemnon "Aga" Atrides, a wealthy Houston businessman, CEO of Atrides Oil and Gas.

Menelaus Atrides, Agamemnon's brother and business partner.

Helen Leda Swann, Menelaus' wife and former archeology graduate student.

Chryseis Lightman, Agamemnon's live-in girlfriend.

Nestor Gibbon, a friend of Achilles' and Agamemnon's and retired Rice University professor of history and classics.

Ajax Gross, a friend of Achilles' from MIT and a NASA engineer.

Ajax Kurtz, another MIT friend of Achilles' and NASA engineer.

Odysseus Laerteson, a friend of Achilles' and Agamemnon's.

Thetis Divine, Achilles' mother.

Idomeneus, a friend of Achilles'.

Machaon Doctorson, Agamemnon's internist.

Eurybates, a friend of Odysseus'.

Meriones, a friend of Agamemnon's and Menelaus'.

Phoenix, a friend of Achilles' and his family.

Hector and his Friends and Allies

Hector "The Hammer" Martillo, an Iraq veteran, scion of the Martillo family, executive vice president of Martillo Interests.

Priam "El Rey" Martillo, Hector's father and founder and CEO of Martillo Interests.

Paris Alejandro "Alex" Martillo, Hector's brother and proprietor of a fashionable hair salon.

Mestor Martillo, Hector's brother who works in the family business.

Cassandra "Cassie" Martillo, Hector's sister and a volunteer at the Jung Center of Houston.

Aeneas, a friend of Hector's.

Vincent "Vinny" Agenor, a friend of the Martillo family and a wealthy securities trader.

Ekheklos, Vinny Agenor's son.

Euphorbus, a friend of the Martillo family.

Othryoneus, Cassandra's out-of-town suitor.

The Gods and Goddesses

Aphrodite "Dite" Cythera, owner of Boutique Cythera.

Apollo Fuente De La Luz, owner of Café Apollo.

Athena Sapienza, Achilles' inner voice and friend from childhood, a polymath, and owner of a small consulting firm.

Poseidon, a presence who lives in Thetis' fountain.

Ares, an ex-boxer and Houston businessman.

Pentha, Ares' teenage daughter and leader of a teenage gang.

The Amazons, Pentha's gang of teenage girls.

THE HOUSTILIAD

An *Iliad* for Houston

BOOK I. MAYHEM IN THE PARK

ARGUMENT. The mood is set—as Alexander Pope might have—by a short section in heroic couplets, which inform the reader that the mythic and the unconscious are the real basis of Achilles' story, and therefore of ours as well. Next we meet our hero. Raised in River Oaks, an exclusive neighborhood in Houston, Achilles is an MIT-trained engineer who has dropped out and lives in Montrose, the most eclectic neighborhood in Houston, with Patroclus, his white macaw, and his girlfriend Briseis. He rides an old BMW motorcycle with a sidecar, and, spoiling for trouble late one afternoon, he and Patroclus head for the park. There they encounter Mestor Martillo and his wife. Mestor is a son of Priam "El Rey" Martillo, the restaurant magnate, and Hector's brother, scion of the Martillo family. The couple asks Achilles to take their picture. He obliges. Then he slashes Mestor, kills him, takes his Rolex, and abducts his wife. He drives her north and finds a remote spot off a Farm to Market road, where he beats and rapes her and then kills her. Patroclus pecks out her eyes. Achilles sears the body clean of evidence with a blowtorch and melts her iPhone with its GPS tracking. He and Patroclus head home. Poseidon, who lives in a fountain in the yard of Achilles' mother, sends a storm to wash her body into a bayou and clean Mestor's of any traces of Achilles. At home Achilles gloats to Patroclus that they are in the clear and hoses down the sidecar. In a moment of remorse, he confronts Athena, his muse and mentor, who emerges from his unconscious. He blames his actions on the goddess, who, he claims, has deserted him. He is emphatic: He will not atone.

Achilles' wrath is where our tale begins
then spools out venom and men's mortal sins.
It's tempered true yet riffs on Homer's style,
suffused with guile, grit, and mordant wile.
The enterprise is underpinned by myth—
Achilles' soul and psyche are the plinth
on which our story's force and verve depend,
and which the meddling gods and Fate upend.
Men savage men in violent travails
though in the end it's humor that prevails.
        Athena, alive within his soul, takes umbrage—
our hero lacks all decency and homage:

Achilles, haunched by his bike and sidecar,
the white macaw, Patroclus, on his shoulder—
two omnivores intent on prey—the man
and bird now scan the scene for drunks and strollers.
Their hopes for booty fade as darkness nears,
but twilight's maw disgorges easy marks.
        "Say, Mister, can you take a shot of us?"
His wife obliges, hands her iPhone to him.
        "Do it. Do it," and Patroclus whistles.
The hauncher straightens, "Say cheese, eternity
would best remember happy, smiling faces."
        Click, click, click, click, click,
five shots from which to choose. He grins then smirks.
        "Thanks, Mister . . . Mister?" says the Rolex man.
        "Achilles Peleuson. I'm glad to be of help."
        "You mind my asking what you do for work?
I'm guessing there is more to you than this,"
the well-stacked woman says. "I'm curious."
        "The parrot, what's his name?" the husband asks.
        "Patroclus, Bird of Paradise, and as

for me, a lot of things. I hope you like
the shots."
        "You're kind, Achilles, to take so many pics."

        "Do it. Do it."
                "Shush, Patroclus, quiet,
I'll do it when I'm good and ready."
                        "Now,
I'm really curious, so what's your work?"
She looks at him, inviting, ripe and ready.
        "The Bird of Paradise, surprising handle,
I admire campy humor."
                "Do it."
        "Do what? He seems insistent," the looker says.
        "He's special, Patroclus is a trooper, a friend."
He nape-kisses the bird and laughs. "You want
to feed Patroclus? Take this." He grabs a hunk
of ground-up chuck and wads an eyeball shape,
then drops it in her hand. She's drenched in fear.
"He's gentle, hold it out and watch him take it."
        At once the raptor flares, snaps up the meat
and nicks her hand. "My God, he's quick and mean."
        This time her husband asks, "What do you do?"
        "I don't do much. We travel some, you know,
the Alamo, the Little Bighorn, in town
the San Jacinto Monument, gun shows
across the country, soon a trip up East
to visit Gettysburg and Washington,
the Vietnam Memorial, then home."
        "And so what do you do for work? I mean."
        Why raise my family money, River Oaks
or mention engineering, MIT?
"In fact, Patroclus is the secret. I sleep

with rich, good-looking widows unless he's jealous
and win at pool and poker, roll some drunks
if they look prosperous. And hold up yokels
if they engage my interest."

                    "Do it. Do it."

The biker's big, well-muscled. He glints and glares,
then reaches down and hefts a tire iron.

    "Hold on, the Rolex you can have, my wallet.
Whatever else you want. I beg you, please."

    Her mouth is clotted, a knock-off of "The Scream."

    "I beg you, leave my wife and I alone."

    "I must. When people beg for mercy, none
should be forthcoming. Honor dies with begging."

    "You're crazy, from some creepy movie. This
can't happen here. No way. We're leaving now."

    Then fierce Patroclus rages in his face
and stills him upright—stopped dead in his tracks.
Achilles catches the Rolex arm, then brings
the tire iron smartly down and rips out
his cheek and jaw. A second blow midships
the temple spills his brains in creamy florets
and sucks him through the black hole of forever.

"Do it. Do it," Patroclus whistles. "Do it."

    The Biker grabs the breasty woman, lifts
her, stuffs her in the sidecar. "Say one word,
you're dead." He holds Patroclus in one arm,
nape kisses him, speeds north, and kills his lights,
turns off a quiet Farm to Market road,
then lurches through the rutted dirt and cuts
the engine at a copse of oak and scrub.

    "You scream, you die, that clear?" He binds her with
some bungee cords and laughs. "I'll be with you

in just a moment, Ma'am." Quite courtly, no?
　　"Do it. Do it. Shag her."
　　　　　　　　"Quiet, Bird."
　　He rolls a condom on. *Goddamn forensics,*
anyway—he'd watched TV, the crime shows.
"It's show time, little lady. Here it comes."
He smartly breaks one mandible and then
the other. Rapes her through and through. Now spent,
and limp, he leers. "Say cheese, your children need
to see their mother happy. Please, a smile."
He forces the tire iron past the jaw
that cannot clench. With one emphatic push,
he thrusts it through the palate up and home
to cauliflower. It is a second coming.
"Patroclus, your turn. You've more than earned it. Go."
　　The raptor warrior rages, mounts her, pecks
her eyes out, gulps them like Achilles' chuck.
The Biker takes her phone (*what if it has*
my picture on it?), opens a saddle bag
and pulls a blowtorch from it, melts the phone
(and its transponder) to a stew and fires
the iron molten to free it of her flesh,
then burns his semen in the milky bag.
He singes her to burn off traces of
his DNA—flares off her hair as well.
Testosterone now surges through their blood,
Achilles, dispatcher, sated, shining darkness,
his friend Patroclus, Bird of Paradise.
Toward home the tires hum hosannas and
hallels.

　　At once Poseidon comes alive.
Solidified within a fountain deep
in River Oaks, he sallies from the yard

of Thetis, Achilles' mother and protector.
Conspiracies between the gods and men
sometimes begin this way—recall Achilles
was the offspring of a man and goddess.
His need for help impelled the trident master:
that night Poseidon, Brawler, Squaller, sent
a rain of terror from the Gulf to wash
away his traces from the Rolex man.
Then north it blew so fiercely that the runoff
dumped her body in a bayou, floated
Achilles free of harm. Poseidon then
returned to moss-encrusted, stony silence.

Achilles and Patroclus shared a house
in Montrose with Briseis near Café
Apollo. His love was out of town with friends,
so bird and man sat on the patio
at breakfast.
        "Want to hear about our caper?
It's right here in the paper. Curious?"
he smugly said one morning two days later.
    "Do it. Do it." Patroclus whistled shrilly.
    "The story says a certain Mestor Martillo—
martillo, some hammer Mestor was, a mere
boychick with a Rolex—was found, his skull
bashed in, his brain destroyed by some blunt tool.
They think it was a robbery gone bad.
The paper says he was a member of
the clan that owns Martillo's restaurants.
He is involved and well-connected, forty.
It mentions Priam 'El Rey' Martillo, his father,
and a brother, Hector, back from Iraq.
Remember him, the Latin with the mouth?
His Rolex is gone, but no cash or rings

are missing, and no credit cards were taken.
His wife has disappeared without a trace
which doesn't fit with robbery alone.
No one has been arrested yet. The police
are short of leads and ask the public's help.
We're home! Home free, the Rolex we can trade
as martial swag—the little pisher's watch,
Mestor and his wife dispatched for booty.
Well, friend, we had a bit of luck—two types
of booty, a Martillo dead to boot.
This afternoon I'll powerwash the sidecar."

Remorse arrived like a summer of crows.
He shooed the birds as if they were the plague,
thought to recall the envoys, then banished them.
    Athena, commissure of my journey, you,
I longed for when I took that woman, raped her.
I only sought your counsel, your consortium.
Athena, you ignored me, so I had her.
Fate dealt me her, her death, my swag, escape.
Return and educate me—lead me out
of impulse, as I writhe naked in the slough.
He closed his eyes and sought the woman he
had known since second grade and always loved—
the woman nested in him by his manhood,
that residue of fire trusted to him,
the boyish, gray-eyed goddess, virgin temptress
whose face and smile surged within him though
a thousand layers down. His psyche's keep
impeded her, not willing to accede
to Cronus' soul-submerging, evil sway,
as if to say, "Bend first to me, renounce
your unchecked rage and I will give you access
to the goddess. Now you cannot hear her."

A riptide of desire had swept him out
to sea, but she remained hard-wired in him,
offline but ready in his circuitry.
I won't atone, I won't. I know it's wrong,
but you deserted me. I'm lost and still
search every pretty face for you, Athena,
commissure and journey—limbic you,
nebulous anchor of clarity, deceit.
He thought, *Look, give it up. The will-o'-the-wisp*
is not worth chasing. There's Briseis waiting.
Why dredge regret up from the swamp?
                              "Patroclus,
Briseis was going straight to work from Austin.
Let's pick our girlfriend up and grab a bite."
"Do it. Shag her," cawed his loving bird.

BOOK II. BRISEIS, THE BEAUTIFUL

ARGUMENT. Agenor, a Martillo family friend, and his cronies relax over drinks after work at BrioBrio, a men's establishment with solicitous hostesses. Achilles' girlfriend Briseis, a University of Texas honors graduate, works there for the thrill as much as the money. She waits on Agenor's table, and as she fills drink orders, he asks her to spend the night with him. When she refuses, he gropes her and she retaliates. Achilles and Patroclus arrive to take her to dinner, and when Achilles discovers what has happened, he threatens Agenor and pins his neck to the floor with his boot. Security intervenes. Achilles, Briseis and Patroclus leave for dinner at Café Apollo. Briseis recounts the incident, and Achilles is furious and supportive. Inwardly he is conflicted and guilty about his own actions with Mestor and his wife and rationalizes that his motives are different from Agenor's. The three head home in a relaxed, playful mood. Later that evening Achilles thanks Athena and Poseidon for helping him deliver Briseis from harm and for his success with Mestor and his wife. Athena is listening and shrewdly assesses his inner life.

After Achilles, Briseis, and Patroclus leave Café Apollo, Ajax Gross and Ajax Kurtz, old friends of Achilles' from MIT, drop by for dinner. Hector sees the two, and Apollo urges him to confront them about Achilles' role in his brother Mestor's death and to mention Achilles' run-in with Agenor. Gross and Kurtz know nothing about Mestor and tell him so. After he leaves they wonder if there is a side to Achilles they don't know and speculate on Hector's motives in provoking them.

Some Fridays after work financial types
would drink at BrioBrio—a cross between
a titty bar and cocktail lounge. They'd come
without their female colleagues, hang around,
imbibe too much, make sotto voce crude
remarks, imagine screwing all that walked—
and most were lookers of the first degree.
Some girls were ready for a price to meet.
And therein lay the problem, so to speak—
these luscious girls in only thongs and pasties
(the look was slightly retro but it worked)
sought late night rendezvous, but not Briseis,
who worked there almost as a lark for fun.
You can depend upon the gods to blur
distinctions. Guests at BrioBrio had
an incandescent lust and too much booze
aboard to figure who was there with sex
for sale and who sold only sultry looks.

A lurid tale unfolded with our hero.
One afternoon Agenor sat with cronies,
the market closed, their cell phones off and holstered.
They drank and shot the shit—asshole buddies,
these comrades in a war of wealth and power.
This hombre was a take-no-prisoners trader,
who fought for clients, made them money, and moved
with ease across a wealthy swath of Houston.
El Rey relied on him to fill his coffers,
and Priam's clan, the restaurateurs, were rich
because of him. This wizard now made small talk
and ogled hostess after hostess—Briseis
first and foremost. The girl Achilles loved,
near topless in a satin thong, served drinks
and worked among the frisky gents. Their tweets

were wicked lewd: *With luck and cash, you bone*
a hooker, a sexy looker of your choice.
You buy it on the hoof, this tender beef.

Briseis worked at BrioBrio only,
too risky mixing power, booze, and sex—
high rollers tipped, and that was it for her.
She did it for the thrill. Her rationale
did not explain her motives: "The pompom squad
at UT Austin and Plan II does not
prepare a girl for much—not engineering,
cosmetic sales or even flipping burgers.
Communications majors have it better
than a booky broad who played hooky
from her economics class to read
pulp fiction, Brontë, Rand, and Margaret Atwood.
For Heaven's sake, a lark is all it is.
Besides, my love, come clean, admit the truth:
you like my working there. It's edgy too,
just what a dropout biker well degreed
from MIT wants in his fated love.
What's more, this girly bird calls forth your worm.
To tell the truth: I like Achilles firm."

At first the scene was cool—men well-behaved,
pretending talk of football, watched the girls.
The problem was Briseis: beauty so
bewitching all but Helen wept in envy.
The girl's magnetic smile could gather a
Mesabi Range of filings, suspend them taut—
erect and pointing north at lust's true pole.
The men were helpless, caught in a boil of blood
and waves of ancient, primal needs that seethed
beneath the crust of social intercourse.

Agenor, blotto, looked her up and down,
"Hey guys, whadaya think of this good-looker?
So honey, what's your name, my foxy lady?"

She smiled and stiffened more than his resolve.

"So tongue-tied you can't answer? Come on, darling.
Not bashful or stuck up I hope."

"It's tough,
my name is 'B.'—my real one's hard to say.
Do you guys need another round of Scotch?"

"I think we're good for now, but what say later
that we go out together, get a bite,
and then go back to my place for some fun."

"I'm sorry, I work strictly here, but thanks."

Not wanting to lose face in front of friends,
Agenor said, "Just name your price to come
with me for dinner and an evening's romp."

"I told you I work only here. That's it."

"So fine you are." He stuffed a C-note in
her thong, just where the strap and frontpiece met.

"Thank you, I'm glad you understand. I'll find
you someone nice. You'll see, you'll really like her."

Half-crazed by booze and playing to the crowd,
he spun her round and groped her crotch.

"You shit,
fuck off. You know the rules. Get lost, you creep."

"That's no way to treat a customer.
I want my C-note back."

"No way, I told
you, fuck off, mister."

"Call me Vinny. Okay?"

"Well, Mister Vinny O'Kay, Irish, I
presume, fuck off." She pulled the C-note out
and took a match then lit the bill and smiled.
She dropped it in his lap. "You're hot as blazes,

Mister O'Kay, I'll say!" and walked away.
  "You big mouth whore, I'll settle scores with you."
  But she was blithely on to other clients,
her black eyes flashing, salacious and serene.
  He wasn't done: "I have a lot of friends
in Houston . . ."
       She yelled at him across two tables,
"Well, I'm not one of them. You're stinking drunk."
  Agenor fumed. Now on his feet, he turned
the table over, hurled a glass at her.
Security was there between the girl
and him in seconds. The customers were cheering.
  "Hey, Mister Vinny Hot Pants, how they hanging?"
one guy in pin stripes yelled and lewdly gestured.

Just then in walked Achilles with Patroclus
and recognized Agenor and his son
Ekheklos from the papers. He saw Briseis,
tight-lipped and teary-eyed, the groper's scowl,
the guards about to clear the room and blew,
"Did he, this motherfucker, fuck with you—
this piece of shit?" and pointed at Agenor.
  "It's okay, the guy was out of line.
Relax, he's drunk. It really is okay."
  "You stupid pussy, it's not okay with me.
He doesn't scare me, this big shot friend of yours."
  Achilles said, "I should. You're meat, you asshole."
  "Oh, yeah, let's see. There're five of us and you."
  And then it was a scene from *Blazing Saddles*.
Agenor kicked Achilles in the shins
and lunged. The biker juked aside and laughed.
Agenor fell face down.
      "Some tough guy you are.
Now put your puss to work and mop the floor."

Achilles' boot heel graced his twisted nape
to mark his conquest. "I could snap your neck
and end your problems now, you stupid fuck."
　　"Do it. Do it," raged Patroclus.
　　　　　　　　　　　　"Shush."
　　Security broke in and motioned off
Achilles, who backed away, "That's fine, I'll leave
the speeches to my friend here. Come on B.,
let's you and I, Patroclus, leave these shits."
　　And so Achilles, the Avenger, Briseis,
the Beautiful, and their dear Patroclus, Bird
of Paradise, now turned their backs on carnage.
　　"I want to know what happened—how this guy
got out of line with you," Achilles said.
"He'll hear from me, I promise, if it's bad.
Let's talk about it over dinner. You game?
Perhaps Café Apollo. What's your pleasure?"

The Montrose Café was Hector's lair away
from home and sat almost across the street
from Aphrodite's. At her boutique young Alex—
Paris Alejandro, Hector's brother—
would launch a quest that drew in Priam's clan
and allies against the cuckold Menelaus—
sweet Helen's husband—his brother, Agamemnon,
Achilles, and their allies in a feud
that soon would dwarf the Biker's wanton rage.

Disgust is what a person would have felt
if he had heard Briseis summing up
Agenor's crude assault. "He's low life scum,"
she said and scowled.
　　　　　　　　　　Once more he vowed revenge.
He took her face and turned it up, then kissed

her gently on the forehead, lips and eyelids.
His fingers stroked her cheeks. Her black eyes brimmed.
They drank Greek beer and ate fresh-baked moussaka.
He glanced at the Aegean islands, caught
in photos on the wall, and smiled slyly.

     "Look, Crete," he said, "it's shaped like Galveston."
They laughed. A photo of a burnished Troy
was on the wall behind him.

                          Briseis looked
at it. A frown now shadowed her. "What if
events at BrioBrio had gotten out
of hand and drawn in both Agenor's friends
and Hector with the whole Martillo clan
and hired guns? You know what might have happened—
open warfare with vendetta killings,
no peace for anyone for years to come."

     "Not likely, B., I wouldn't worry. Let
me pay the check and we'll unwind a bit
at home."

     But what he couldn't talk about
was Mestor or his wife, her gruesome rape
and murder. Or Briseis. He could not grasp—
at least not consciously—and thus could not
admit that his outraged defense of her
at BrioBrio flowed from darkness so
profound its bleakness masked that in the human
brain, rape and love share pathways, parallel,
entangled—like tracks the trains to Auschwitz used
while others headed West to hope and freedom.
     Where was his guide and friend Athena
when he needed her? *My freighted robes
are death's alone. At times I am his vicar.
No one must ever know my thoughts or deeds.*

What havoc it would wreak if it got out
I murdered Mestor, raped and killed his wife.
What's more, I loved the rush. Damn Athena,
damn her. Who is Briseis, anyway—
embodiment of light? Of love? Athena?
And who was Mestor's wife, the girl I savaged,
whose eyes Patroclus, my white macaw, devoured?

B. held Patroclus in the sidecar—the scene
seemed tender, three at ease, relaxed and happy.
In truth the ride was Mestor's wife redux—
Achilles' limbic surges were the same.
He parked the bike. "Go take a shower B.
and then who knows," he smiled.
                                   Patroclus whistled,
"Do it. Do it. Shag her."
                         Briseis laughed,
"Good idea, you up for that, Achilles?
It's not a question, Big Guy. Ready in five."

So with Briseis safe with him at home
in Montrose, he closed his eyes in gratitude
and pitched his fingers church-like, a decalogue
of tribute to Athena and Poseidon,
nothing less than a *shehecheyanu*—
pieties (both daft and zany) he
believed, sometimes at least, might flow from him.
Athena listened quietly: His prayers
included amnesty for rape and murder.
Thus beasts of every stripe will praise their gods.
How hard to know what really prompted prayers.
This man, Achilles, had more facets than
a thousand heroes, Buckminsterfullerenes,
and constellations multiplied together.

He's not prepared for what he needs to own:
his journey's ghosts lodged next to him as baggage.
The sidecar held his friendships, lusts, and loves.
Patroclus, victims, and Briseis slowed
the hero's pace, caused him to oversteer
the bike, retrace terrain he'd covered, return
devoid of plenty, without the grace he craved.
Achilles' fault was not his heel but need
of maps, deliberate in their roads and contours.
His rage set him adrift, impoverished him,
as did what passed for love and really was
enchantment by Briseis and a bird.

No one could figure who killed Hector's brother.
No clues emerged, no motives. The police declared
that it was random—wrong guy, wrong place, wrong time.
The search for Mestor's wife was fruitless too.
She vanished as if swallowed by the sea.

That night Achilles' comrades Ajax Gross
and Ajax Kurtz stopped by Café Apollo.
(The Biker and his birds had long since flown.)
    Achilles had attracted them to Houston.
Good jobs, intrigue, and mischief kept them there.
They'd met at MIT when Ajax Gross,
the first boat stroke, recruited him to row.
Achilles made the eight as well. They buoyed
the shell, attracted Ajax Kurtz as cox,
and almost won a first place medal in
the eights the weekend of the Charles Regatta.
By day they worked at NASA—engineering
and astrophysics applied to rocketry.
Their weekends were a different wizardry.
    And now they wandered in for drinks and dinner.

The Hammer spotted them, and Apollo egged
the hothead on, "Ask them about Achilles.
The Biker's friends are surely in the loop."

And so he menaced them before they found
a table.

Then blind with anger, booze, and grief,
the ex-marine began to rant, "Your friend's
a rogue. He coolly killed my brother Mestor
in Hermann Park. I want to know what happened.
So out with it."

"Look, Hector, we're in the dark.
You have no reason to suspect him. Pure
conjecture is what I'm hearing," Gross replied.

"The BrioBrio shit. You can't deny
he brutalized Agenor for no cause."

"BrioBrio—we don't know any details.
I bet the story has another side.
Agenor is no innocent. And Mestor,
I don't know what happened to your brother,
and you don't either. Sober up, go home.
There's nothing that we know, I promise you."

"I want an answer now if you don't want . . ."

"Look, take your swagger elsewhere or there's trouble,"
and Gross and Kurtz edged toward the bleary boozer.

And there it ended for the present—Ajax
confused, Hector suffused with hate and booze,
still spoiling for a fight he could not win.
When he had gone, they looked at one another
and struggled with the news of Mestor's death.
Both wondered silently about Achilles.
Was there a side to him they had not seen?

"Perhaps honor is what's eating Hector—
and pride. He thinks he owes it to his kin
to settle scores," a puzzled Kurtz surmised.

"He has no proof of murder. It's speculation.
It might be Mestor who attacked Achilles,
and nothing ties our brother to the scene.
If he and Mestor fought, and I say 'if,'
this Mestor may have taunted him or struck
first blows. And who's to blame? Our friend is wild,
I'll grant you that. He's got an outsized rage.
But murder? No way his trigger temper equals
murder. If they met and egos soared
and spun beyond control, who says the fault's
Achilles'? I don't believe it for a second.
Were there harsh words? An ugly brawl? Perhaps.
But murder? I bet self-defense. Again,
only Hector puts him at the scene."

Events across the street tomorrow will make
the Hammer fume and sizzle with desire,
and Mestor's death will seem a minor blip,
as Aphrodite stirs the pot and lures
sweet Helen to the bed of brother Paris,
the bon vivant of the Martillo clan.
Again, it is the gods in their pursuit of pleasure
who nudge their world toward Armageddon's brink.

BOOK III. BOUTIQUE CYTHERA

ARGUMENT. We meet Aphrodite who owns Boutique Cythera on Westheimer, a chic establishment that caters to adventuresome River Oaks types and the hip of Montrose. A mystical presence hangs over the shop, which seems in service to her beauty. Her friend Paris Alejandro Martillo, Alex, comes by ostensibly to shop; his hair salon is closed for the day because of a burst water main. He tries to entice Aphrodite into an affair. She nixes the idea and suggests that if he is looking for love, he meet Helen Leda Swann, a rich, young River Oaks matron, whose husband Menelaus and his brother Agamemnon run a large oil company. At first he demurs but eventually warms to the idea. Aphrodite, out of sympathy for her friend and a love of mischief, sends Helen to his salon for a cut. Their relationship starts slowly, but as Helen points out, it must develop—she has written her masters thesis on the excavation of Troy and knows the story well.

Boutique Cythera was a pricy shop
for well-heeled matrons and trendy Montrose types.
Aphrodite Cythera, known as Dite
to her friends, was founding spirit
of the gauzy, tryst-sustaining place
across the street Café Apollo graced.
She sold expensive dresses, intimate
apparel, and high-end costume jewelry.
The brilliant custom bra designer quipped,

"The human form can use a little boost."
She put this on her business card and deadpanned,
"My bras uplift the body and the soul."

The dreamy space defined a realm apart—
and Aphrodite's reign was absolute,
but nuanced. Her presence hung unnamable,
alluring as the sea—Ionia
transported to the cases, rows, and racks
of Montrose. Subtle shades of peach and orange
prevailed but anchored by an earthy teak
which fostered forest sprites and even dybbuks—
you felt the presence too of Artemis,
though Aphrodite clearly was sole author—
her rule was deft but firm and moved this world
to passion and ensuing action. She glowed
a beauty so electric it became
the standard that made Houston women weep,
effaced the face of Beatrice, and left
the two Egyptians, ageless Cleopatra
and peerless Nefertiti, also-rans.
She turned Athena's lovely mien and Hera's
to unbecoming sharpness. Paris' choice
as we look back was obvious—not sky,
nor sea, nor gods, no force of nature serves
except to say, All women fall away.

She was surprised one ordinary morning.
Her old friend Alex—Paris Alejandro,
Priam's son and Hector's brother—seemed
to happen in by chance. Martillos were
in business—restaurants, a dozen deals
that stretched the limits of the law—and prospered
in the shadows. All but he and Cassie—

Cassandra, the Jung Center volunteer
par excellence and jaunty Alex, who owned
a hair salon on Upper Kirby that coiffed
the rich and corporate wives (and paramours).
So everyone who counted knew the place.
Sly Alex helped them primp for balls and trips
and bedded more than one at his apartment.
Discretion was his byword—no taint attached
to him except that many thought him gay
because of his profession. He always smiled
a randy smile at these abetting rumors.

He wandered in, and seeing no one there,
he poked around the mannequins, admired
the bras and lingerie, and caught a hint
of Dite's presence in the air. He held
a pair of lacy panties.

          Then she blurted
from behind and startled him, "Good taste!
What lucky lass is destined for this gift,
this dainty bit of my boutique? Someone
I know?"

      "No one."

          "Bullshit, Alex, which bed-
bound vixen are you shopping for? I know
their sizes, all of them. I'll make them fit."

    "My, Dite, so quick to come to closure. No one.
I'm here by chance, so can the cutting cant.
Some quirky goad delivered me today,
some wisp of who knows what has guided me
to you."

      "Your turn to can it, Alex. Men
are so transparent. What gives?"

          "Trust me, nada.
I had to close the shop. A main has burst.

There's water everywhere on Kirby, and Fate
has sent me for a visit."
                                "You hang too much
with Cassie. You believe that trash of hers?
Don't answer. You do a line this morning, Alex?"
    "No, no, I'm always clean till after six."

He looked at her, the sunlight in her hair,
the sea in his amygdala, his being
freighted with her beauty. He could smell
her sex as steamy as Cythera. An
inferno of desire seared him. *Just ask
her out. The crucible is yours to fire.*
    The goddess, knowing everything, had sensed
his mood, "You hitting on me, Alex? Come clean."
    "Is that so bad? I've always fancied you?"
    I'm going to have a little fun with this,
thought Aphrodite. *It's my due as goddess.*
    "Well, yes and no. You know my reputation.
I'm with a guy a month and then it's over.
We're friends, let's keep it there, no more."
                                "Your face
is peerless. Acolyte kazoos should praise
your beauty! Then tambourines and trumpets. Tell me?"
    *Where does he get this crap? I bet he took
creative writing classes at UH.*
    "Very cute, but no, it's not a go.
We'd scrap and kill each other in a week.
But friends are friends—I'd like to help you find
a woman suitable for love." *But truth
be told, I'll sow a little mischief too,*
she thought. Then lewdness overtook her plans.
*"Love" and "evil," are near anadromes.
I'll lead him on a bit and see what happens.*
"Again, it's love not marriage that you seek?"

He nodded. "I have a customer, a lass
of stabbing beauty, Helen, charming and
discreet, a woman restless in her marriage.
She's hinted that she's bored with Menelaus.
They're rich and live in River Oaks. Together,
her husband and his brother Agamemnon
hold vast reserves of oil around the world,
so money's not the issue. I'm sure of that.
The woman's tethered, ripe, and zesty—ready
for adventure. I'm never wrong. Trust me.
I think your playfulness and verve will draw
her out. Use the line about kazoos—
it's wacky, crisp, and quick, just right in tone
without the ooze of serious intent.
You'll see. Bizarre *bon mots* appeal to her.
At home she's in a prison of convention,
stifled by him. It's right, I promise. What say?"

    "Look, Dite, something guided me to you
this morning. Some force I can't explain and now
wants us to be a pair. Can you not feel
the current?"

            "Alex, poor boy, get real. We would
dismember one another in a heartbeat.
Yes, we could get it on, but keep it on?
Never. You have to trust me. Helen's right."

    "Dite, I'd hate to miss a chance with you.
You're wrong, I know you're wrong, so listen . . ."

                          "No,
no. Absolutely not. No, Alex, no."

    "You're one tough broad. . . . You win. . . . Uncle, tell me."

    "Look, Alex, I know my customers, and you,
my picky friend, will not be disappointed.
She's coming for a fitting later. I'll
direct the conversation cautiously

to love and probe her state. I'll try it out.
I'll warm her up and send her by your shop.
I promise you'll know what to do from there."
      She kissed him on the cheek and sent him packing.

The goddess made a stir-fry of his brain:
his man thing crackled—the pop excited him.
How strange he hadn't heard of her, this Helen,
but who knew more of love than Aphrodite?
No client ever mentioned her, but really
you could never tell. He searched the web—
no LinkedIn, not on Facebook. Yes, discreet.
Yet bit-by-bit he pieced it all together—
born Helen Leda Swann and four years married,
her husband twenty years her senior, raised
in Dallas, Randolph-Macon, Junior League,
museum boards, some charities, a life
predictable, but here, yes, here was something—
a master's in antiquities, a year
in Asia Minor digging out a tell
at Troy. Does Aphrodite know this part?
He needed no convincing. *This could work.*
      He called her, "Dite, I'm in. When she arrives,
sell it. I'd like to meet this Helen chick."

The goddess started coolly probing things
at home, the moods of Menelaus, his nights
away, his waywardness, and then without
a hint she raised the notion of romance.
She knew the perfect guy who kept a secret,
was fun and kind, good looking too. "My plan
deserves a try. He's someone you can trust."
      Now caught off guard, the woman hesitated.
She looked perplexed, both anxious and unsure.

Helen had been involved before but not
so close to home. She frowned and then she brightened:
"Okay, I'll let him cut my hair and see
if things progress from there, no promises,
except to keep an open mind. If he
is nice, presentable and has a bit
of flair . . . we'll see. . . ."

"That's fair. A thought—I have
a present for you. Something to help your tryst
along." She handed her the lacy panties
that Alex fairly panted over. "Go try
them on and tell me what you think."

Next thing
there was a giggle, then a throaty scream,
"My God, they're great. I hope I like this guy!"

You know what happened next. How can you not?
She visited his shop and liked his style.
"You're right about this guy," she purred to Dite.
"I had him cut my hair and blow it out,
but nothing's happened, not a word from him.
You think he's going to make a move or not?
I hate to waste his talent on my husband."
"Be patient. He works carefully, you'll see."

Young Alex loved the look he had created:
no mortal woman is more lovely than
this Helen I have fashioned for myself.
I'll let her build a head of steam and see
if I can bring the goddess' booty home.

A few days later Helen called on pretext.
"There is a dinner at my husband's club.
Can you fit a blow dry in today?

Perhaps my hair could do with teasing too."

"Of course. No problem. What's your cell in case
we need to change the time?"

Pure cock-and-bull.

Once there, he pampered her and stroked her hair
beyond propriety. His breath was just
a Zephyr of a whisper as he combed
her out, "Can we have lunch next week? I'll call."

Our Alex knew the hideaways as well
as any escort. He phoned and got voice mail.
I better wait for her. What if her hub
is jealous and monitors her calls? At last
she answered. After pleasantries, he started,
"How bout a low-key lunch sometime next week?"
I'll gig her with her dig of Troy, he thought.
"I know a quiet, unassuming place—
as safe as Thrace for Aphrodite's tryst
with Ares. Sorry, lunch is all I have
in mind, of course."

"Okay, I'll bite. What's that
supposed to mean?"

"It's south off NASA Road.
It has a good crab salad, shrimp, and snapper.
You would enjoy yourself."

"Of course . . . I'll come."

"Don't worry. No one we know will see us there.
It's way outside the circles you inhabit."

"I'll trust you on the food. Where is this place?"

"Go south on 45, at NASA Road
turn east, and down a ways, and almost at
the water there's a crab shack called The Launch.
Say one o'clock."

"I'm looking forward to it."

(What Alex couldn't know is Ajax loved

the food and lunched there once a month at least.
It's good to have a goddess kosher acts
to save your bacon in a tryst—thus Gross
was gone, but just, that fateful afternoon.
Most things aren't rocket science for the gods.)

A simple unassuming lunch of crab,
white wine, and glancing looks were all it took
to hook their talons deep into each other
and unleash a hurricane of rage
that would engage Achilles, Hector and
their allies, not to mention Menelaus
and his brother, sullen Agamemnon,
in self-destructive, viscous, mortal combat.

A second lunch was followed by a kiss—
no more. And then a third, a fourth. Soon Helen
began to doubt the strength of his libido.
He peppered her with queries of the dig
at Troy that went back fifteen years.
                                        This boy
cannot be serious about a tryst.
I'm a woman wearing Aphrodite's
panties. Maybe he's gay and faking it.
        "So tell me, Helen," he started in again,
"I've read there're many levels to the dig.
I'm wondering if ancient Greeks and Trojans
contended there at all, or is it just
a series of middens, jumbles of Hittite shards
and ancient ruins capped by Roman coins?"
        She cleared her throat, "The arguments go back
and forth. The story's the important thing,
not facts—how myth is shadow to our lives."
        "I see. Then your opinion is . . ."
                                        "Please, stop."

She stroked his hand and placed it on her breast.
"Our names alone ensure a love supreme,
as jazzy as the coolest Harlem dive.
You have no choice—the story must go on.
So take me home and do me. Do me right.
And right by me as well—unless you want
to face disgrace in Houston, which is sure
to come if you deny the story's course
and fail. You will be thought a flaccid fraud
and impotent unlike those ballsy Houston
business types that make the city run."

BOOK IV. A MEETING OF THE MINDS

ARGUMENT. The relationship between Helen and Alex intensifies. One day Chryseis, Agamemnon's live in girlfriend, becomes suspicious when she accompanies Helen to Boutique Cythera to go shopping: She suspects Helen's purchases are not to please her husband Menelaus. She tells Agamemnon, who shares her suspicions with his brother, and the three set out on what Agamemnon dubs "Operation Desdemona Lite," an attempt to document Helen's infidelity. Helen parries their efforts, but a fashion blogger posts a picture of Alex and an unnamed client at lunch, whom Chryseis recognizes as Helen. When confronted, Helen says lunch with her hairdresser is proof of nothing. Certain of her guilt, Agamemnon and Menelaus ponder their next steps. They think about enlisting Achilles but worry he cannot be trusted. By chance Nestor Gibbon, a retired history professor with a brilliant mind, calls Agamemnon to catch up. When Agamemnon learns that Nestor has been invited to an informal get together Achilles' house, he asks him to get him an invitation as well. Achilles, Briseis, and their friends sit around drinking and chatting. Achilles grimly observes Agamemnon's infatuation with Briseis. Nestor tells a long boring story which everyone pans. A series of preposterous opera jokes ensues, and the evening ends without Agamemnon's having a clearer understanding of Achilles' state of mind. After people leave, a love scene between Achilles and Briseis reveals a tender, philosophical side of Achilles, but, as Athena listens, the ledger remains unbalanced because Achilles does not tally the killings of Mestor and his wife.

The two were not a number yet, but that's
where it was headed—quiet lunches outside
the Loop and carnal afternoons at his
apartment. They worked hard to keep it light.
  As Helen later said, "It was quite pleasant,
a sweet diversion from my drab routine.
Of course, he's fiery, exciting, a Latin lover
and honestly, compared to Menelaus,
a bull in bed. To me it was as harmless
as a spa when I look back on it."

Nothing would have happened had they remained
discreet, confined their tryst to afternoons
alone or secret New York rendezvous.
A crack developed slowly by bad luck—
not luck but Aphrodite's meddling scheme:
at her behest a craving gnawed at Helen
for clothes she stocked at her boutique in Montrose.
In popped the matron for a bustier
and hose, a thong to please her lover Alex—
she stashed the garments in his spare room dresser
as private markers of their joyous fling,
its titillations.
    Slowly the affair
took on a new dimension—dinner out
if Menelaus had gone to Austin for
the night or slept in Kemah on his yacht—
let's not inquire what kept him occupied.
They ate at restaurants in the Heights or Thai
or other ethnic spots with no cachet—
out of the way with no attendant risk.
They chanced an Austin visit with its bars
and music scene—South By Southwest was on.
It lit a flame that Menelaus had all

but quenched. The two went tubing on the Brazos
when business took her husband to New York.
Each dared the other to screw in every bed
in Texas. Passion swept away their lives.

By chance one morning she and Agamemnon's
tart Chryseis, who lived in his garage
apartment and was on good terms with her—
not sister close as they did not confide,
but cordial, say, polite acquaintances—
went girly shopping at Boutique Cythera.
(Clytemnestra, Agamemnon's wife,
lived in the Virgin Islands, happy to be
rid of him.) Chryseis, a preacher's daughter,
lived delectably in sin. Morals,
the girl explained, were optional, a guide
for others, strictures from her Christian past.
Go figure. Agamemnon was not her first.
At any other store no harm would have
befallen Helen. As she shopped, Chryseis
caught the chemistry between the two.
She must be shopping for some studly guy,
and surely not her husband, thought Chryseis,
and Dite has worked with her before. What's more,
she knew that Menelaus made the rounds.
No frilly lace can lure him back to her.
She's up to something sly. Chryseis' shit
detector was better than a pig's for truffles.
　　　　She held her thoughts and one day adroitly raised
the issue of a yellow cardigan
and then politely asked about a bra
and matching lacy panties.
　　　　　　　　　　　Helen smiled,
"I want my wardrobe spicy for my husband."

Chryseis didn't buy it. *He is self-centered,*
distracted by affairs and work. He loves
his trophy wife but only for the glitz.
Unsure of what to do, the girl applied
first principles: A man's not hard to read.
This doxy knows the score with Menelaus.
She's shopping for the pleasure of some lover.
Chryseis saw through Menelaus' bluster,
his bullshit ploys like sports and business, poker—
though scars and deeper fears, his paltry ego
were hidden from her by her Christian past.

Athena captured all of this but held
her own ideas close. *Poor Menelaus,*
he struts and suffers—alone and terrified.
Outside of business, he is stunted, lives
the desiccated life of many men—
a man in times when gods no longer walk
the earth or venture down with help or succor.
His cringing terror puts him beyond all reach.

Chryseis stewed on Helen's poised response.
What course to take? Could she be absolutely
sure of what she sensed? Or did her mind
play tricks? Would sneering Agamemnon call
her dizzy, ditzy, daft or dumb? With him
you couldn't figure. Moody and hair-triggered,
he might blame her for Helen's roaming ways.
Expecting him to rage, she chose a moment
after sex before booze seized his senses.
She swallowed, screwed her courage up, explained
to him his brother had, might have, a problem.
    "What proof have you of anything illicit
is what I want to know. It's not *Othello,*"

Aga said. "We can't barge in and claim
adultery because she bought some clothes."

The girl was calm, "Let's put it to the test.
You know she bought a yellow cardigan,
quite smart, distinctive. If it's at home, I may
be wrong. If not, she better have a story
to explain the missing sweater. We'll watch
her face to see if she betrays a lie."

"Well, it's a plan. I'll try it out on him,
see what my brother says. Good God, Chryseis,
if this is true, we'll send her back to Dallas
so bruised she'll seem the whore she surely is.
Hold on, it's not fair to come to closure.
We need a neutral name with gravitas
conveying urgency but playful. How's this,
'Operation Desdemona Lite'?"

Aga pulled no punches with his brother,
"It's Helen. Someone may be balling her."

"You're shitting me. A tart behind my back?
Is that conniving bitch a fucking ho?"
It spewed like lava from her husband's mouth.
He put aside all notion of due process,
certain she'd stabbed him in the groin and made
him cuckold. The charges, still unproven, drove
mistrustful Menelaus mad. "So I
propose that you and I, Chryseis too,
confront her, call her out on her behavior.
The cardigan is key. I'll check. It might
be simple. If it's in her closet . . . she's still
on the hook. Is there a hint of who
the bastard is?"

"Look, Menelaus, now
it's just conjecture. There's no evidence,
no smoking gun, no guy to implicate.

Operation Desdemona Lite
should set this sordid matter right. Like you,
I think there's little chance she's faithful, true."
But Shakespeare may have got it wrong: Who says
the poet's hanky is not a sign of panky?

When Helen was confronted, she was cool,
so Menelaus, Aga, and his ho
stood mute a moment, stopped by Helen's aura.
    Chryseis started casually, "By the way,
the cardigan I liked on you so much,
that looked so good. I haven't seen you wear
it."
    Helen did not miss a beat, "I took
it back. It wasn't right. It made me fat.
So what's the deal with you, and why the look?"
    "No deal, it was becoming on you, sexy—
perhaps too sexy."
                  "Too sexy? Really? What's that
supposed to mean? Is there some problem here?"
    "It's nothing really, Helen, but . . . I don't
believe your story. I think you're hiding something."
    "So what don't you believe? Am I on trial?"
    "That you returned the sweater."
                        "Call and check,
you nasty bitch."
              "I saw the looks between
you two—yeah, Dite's helping you advance . . .
oh, I don't know . . . some affair or tryst.
My vibes are rarely wrong on things like this.
I think you're seeing someone."
                        "So you talked
to Aga and my husband? You filthy slut."
At once all motion stopped. The room went still—
as if a poisoned crow fell limp and died . . .

and then was resurrected with a vengeance:
"And you, dear husband, where do you get off
accusing me of infidelity?
Your silence says that you believe the bitch.
It is a groundless, ugly accusation.
A sweater, a missing sweater that she thought
I bought to please a nonexistent lover.
That's what it's about. She thought, you thought,
and Aga. Is this fidelity's reward?

Operation Desdemona Lite
relentlessly crept forward. Like a glacier's
crush it ground down every chance of Fate
or reason's intervening. Menelaus
still could have set it right. A lass like Helen
was sensible and might have come to harbor
if given kindness, love, and decency.

Though Helen had no chance to warn her friend,
cool Dite took Chryseis' call serenely,
" . . . Yes, of course, she returned the cardigan."
        Too bad, Chryseis, anger Aphrodite
and pay a price. The goddess made a note
to get her out of Aga's bed and send
her home disgraced, unsalable, and sullied.
        The troika failed to bring fair Helen down.
For you, salacious reader, here's the deal:
The wife's revenge was pleasure for young Alex
in ways her hub could not imagine, Chryseis
did not know, and Agamemnon longed for.
The three would never know the wiles of love
that Aphrodite taught so well to Helen.

At lunch bad luck soon struck the happy couple—
a blogger of the fashion scene caught them

with chopsticks raised and laughing over sushi.
He snapped a shot and posted it with others.
The title: "Alex Martillo relaxes with
a client." In fairness, it was one of several
candid shots that featured chic salons
much in the eye of Houston's rich and trendy.
Bad luck—Chryseis and her friends saw it.
    When Menelaus confronted Helen with
a copy, she said, "It's proof of lunch, that's all.
We went for sushi following a perm,
that's it."
        Her husband was incensed. What were
his options? Not to allow her out alone?

They had no proof of anything beyond
a lunchtime photo and a missing sweater.
Unsure of what to do, wronged Menelaus
picked up the phone and called his brother.
                           "So here

is a beginning," Aga answered. "First,
we'll act as if it's true, but cautiously.
We've got to think this through, and once we do,
we'll need some muscle, perhaps Achilles. But wait,
I'm too out front on this."
                  "You really are."
    "But, Menelaus, we can't do this alone.
Imagine us in black, behind some gate,
and breaking in, confronting Helen's lover
with guns in hand. We can't do that, not us.
We need an agent with a taste for blood
to beat that motherfucker to a pulp.
The vexing issue is what to do with Helen,
and how to find this guy—or guys, could it
be more than one?—who's balling your sweet wife?

We're stymied till we find the guy she's screwing,
and that, dear brother, will require luck.
　　"For now let's focus on an operative,
someone on the ground with pluck and savvy
who we can trust. A guy who's tough and smart.
For that, my money's on Achilles. I know . . ."
　　Menelaus balked at this: "Don't trust
this guy. You can't control that biker. No chance.
He lives by different rules or lack of rules
and stands for nothing we believe or value.
Don't think about the high school boy, the kid
our children knew and played with. MIT
and Boston, Montrose, drugs have changed the guy."
　　"Who else is there? I think he's our best shot,
much better than a drug cartel assassin
or drifter from a curbside labor pool.
We'll hold him in reserve till we know who
we're after. Then we'll turn his fury loose."

Should fortune, Fate or gods take credit for
Professor Nestor Gibbon's call to chat
with Aga? Here was a chance to gather data,
to probe Achilles' present state of mind.
The Biker had invited some close friends
including Nestor in for camaraderie,
to shoot the shit, a way of catching up
without agendas. Nestor knew no more,
except Achilles planned a kickback evening.
　　"Think you can wangle me an invitation?"
　　"I'll call, find out what I can do. What piques
your curiosity about him now?"
　　"I simply want to see who he's become. . . ."
　　"Good luck, my friend, it's not an easy task.
No one really knows him. He's a cipher.

You'll find Achilles out of phase—perhaps,
not crazed, but certainly a renegade.
He's like a cave blocked by a stone—his mind
emits no light. His brain's on auto-lockdown.
I have no feeling for his private thoughts.
I don't believe that anybody does,
except perhaps Briseis, and that is doubtful."
  "I think I get it, Nestor, but still I'd like
to come. So let me know if you can swing it."

They sat around relaxed with beer and wine,
some smoking dope—Achilles and Patroclus,
the Ajax boys, Briseis, Agamemnon,
with Nestor and Odysseus. Recluse
Idomeneus had also come. The night
was going well until Achilles saw
the way that Aga looked at B. He hid
a wince. *No good will come of this.* To cheer
his mood, he said to Nestor, "Regale us with
a tale."
  Nestor was retired, had held
a named professorship at Rice, well-liked,
but, how to put it, thorough. He had a Wiki
compendium of facts without the filter.
  "My friends, be careful what you wish for." Groans
from all, as if to say to host Achilles,
that was a dumb-ass thing. Now motor-mouth
will drone and drone and drone. "Achilles, thanks
for asking," and without a second's loss
he said, "Well, it was eighteen sixty-nine,
and Emil Skoda bought a plant in Pilzen
in what is now the Czech Republic . . ."
                    "My God,
come on, cut us some slack. It's Friday night.

I want the CliffsNotes version," Ajax Gross
broke in.

"Let him finish. Go ahead."

"He made a fortune in munitions—they
sold piping, weapons, later autos, Panzers—
not Skoda, but the company he founded. . . ."

Odysseus screwed up his face and pursed
his lips, then gently spoke the thoughts of most,
"Please, Nestor, no one doubts your erudition,
but now is not the time for this. I've got
a stumper, an opera question to amuse
the group." (This man Odysseus is whip-smart
clever. He's clever as a chloroplast—
the organelle in plants. How's that? you ask.
Once, when stupefied by drink, he said,
in answer to a dare to name a thing
no man could do, "Who of us can split
a molecule of water with a photon?")

So here is Mister Chloroplast's brain teaser:
"Whose operas are most tiresome? . . . Some thoughts,
no takers . . . Richard Wagner's, because he cows
you. Then you have to low and grin and bear
it." That one did not win him any friends.

"All right, all right, here's one," Briseis said,
"What was the Dutchman's problem?"

Agamemnon
was leering.

"Someone, please."

So Ajax Gross
responded, "He had no money and could not
go Dutch treat."

"Hold it, no, he was high
and flying," Ajax Kurtz shot back.

More groans.
Briseis laughed, "Both very funny, but no.

He had to take a Senta mental journey
to be saved."
                    "Here's one," Achilles said.
"What's Patroclus' favorite opera role?"
A boozy quiet filled the room. "Hint,
The Magic Flute . . . the parrot, Papageno."
        Big Ajax, "Bullshit, parrot's 'pappagallo'
not 'papageno' in Italian,"
                              Then Nestor,
"You know the opera's German, not Italian.
Mozart made up Papageno. It's puff.
The word's not real. No, Schikaneder coined . . .
        "It counts for friends tonight," Achilles said.
"Odysseus, what say you? Call it for us."
        "No way. I think Patroclus is quite happy
with the joke. Let's let it go at that."
        Except for Agamemnon, spirits soared.
His interest in Achilles lost, he sulked
and eyed Briseis up and down. He craved
her body, and Achilles saw it all.
By midnight everyone was heading home.
        The closing words that wafted out were Nestor's,
". . . Argentina, his name was Witold Gombrowicz . . ."

The guys were gone, the dishes done. Patroclus
slumbered on his dowel. Briseis and
Achilles smooched and cuddled on the couch.
His fingers brushed her cheeks. He kissed her eyes,
and drawing back, he took her hands in his
and paused—the moment held him hostage.
                                    Awash
in love, his balance ebbing fast, he slipped
a bit, then more, fell toward the loamy bottom
of a cloudy stream. What filtered up

and broke to conscious thought he censored out:
the night he drove the tire iron through
the brain of Mestor's wife and let Patroclus
peck her glassy eyes and gobble them.
     Immaculate Athena hung her head.
Surely no god or gods give grace to him.
His moral compass is shattered by his lust.
What wizardry allows Achilles license?
     "I love you as the wind loves rain," he said.
     Briseis clicked her palate with her tongue,
inhaled and turned away, then back, her fetching
look beguiling him. "I want to know
the way the wind loves rain, my love. Tell me."
     "As I love you, the wind loves rain. The rain
dissolves in wind, is borne aloft by it—
an act of each with each—the wind now bearing rain,
the rain borne lambent and diffuse by wind—
a marriage whole as day caught up with night—
quiet moments, funny stories, sex,
a common language. Does this make sense to you?"
     "Of course," she said, "it's perfect sense, so lovely.
I love this side of you. I rarely hear
your singing soul. I know ferocity
and tenderness in you, but I dissolve
each time your inner self breaks through. It's rare
and thrilling . . . makes me proud to be with you.
You are my joy," and she began to sob.
     "It's hard for men to let their feelings out.
I do love you the way the wind loves rain.
It's simple and it's true. However many
faults I have, and they are legion, my love
for you helps balance any ledger." He looked
at her. He was the wind subsuming rain.
They both were teary—fused and whole—in love.

He muffled thoughts of mayhem in the park,
as if he kept two ledgers—in one he tallied
his public face, good deeds, his loves and friendships.
Unentered were the brutal rape and murders.
He kept a full accounting locked away,
in hopes of keeping demon guilt at bay.
Another take puts him beyond Athena:
His guilt was two cells deep. Planaria—
the flatworms—had more self-knowledge than her charge.

BOOK V. THE JEALOUS HUSBAND

ARGUMENT. Helen realizes Menelaus knows she is having an affair with someone and fears that he will physically harm her. Alex offers her shelter and suggests she move in with him. The next morning, caught by passion and fear and with only a twinge of guilt, she empties the safety deposit box she and Menelaus share, taking cash, jewelry, his stock, and her voting stock in the brothers' company, and leaves. The move cripples company operations because her voting stock is needed for a quorum to conduct board business. Menelaus reacts first with sorrow—he had expected more of her. When she condescendingly refuses his attempts at reconciliation, his anger flares. He goes to his brother Agamemnon who suggests a plan to force the return of Helen and their assets. Alex is discarded as a target; the brothers will move against Martillo business interests and enlist Achilles to threaten Hector. Meanwhile Achilles learns that two derelicts claim to have seen him in the park with Mestor. After a bedroom romp, he and Briseis head for Café Apollo with Patroclus for drinks and dinner. Hector also hears the rumor. At Café Apollo, he talks with Apollo, who is revered for his special powers, so when he cautions Hector to bide his time, he momentarily restrains himself. Then he ignores Apollo's advice, heads for Achilles' table, and confronts him about his brother Mestor's murder. Achilles ridicules him, and Hector skulks off. A loopy plan by the brothers to intimidate the Martillos with a letter is laughed off by all but Priam.

"My husband knows about my fling with you.
I mean, he doesn't know it's you, but knows
that something's going on. I worry that
he'll lose it and scared to death he'll beat me if
our thing goes public. A cuckold, ridiculed
behind his back, will stop at nothing to
destroy his mate and scuttle what we have."
She told him everything: the gang of three,
the cardigan, Chryseis' nasty sniping,
and most of all her husband's ugly mood.
> Then Alex spoke to calm her, "Move in with me.
The three of them are in lockstep against you.
Just keep your cool and come. I've got a place
that's plenty big."
> > What if he hadn't said that?
Would she have stayed with husband Menelaus,
gone back to Dallas, or found her own apartment?
No one can say, but she was self-reliant,
and Dite could have bolstered her if needed.
Besides, she felt the fault was wholly his.
> She kept her wits, was poised, remained serene—
as if she'd made at most a slight mistake.
Yes, that's the way to handle Menelaus,
and she repeated to herself there was
no proof and nothing linking them as lovers.
I'll sleep on it. See how I feel tomorrow.

Next morning she was at the bank at nine
and cleaned out everything—the cash, her jewels,
securities, both his and hers, and worst
or best of all—depending on your point
of view—her voting stock, essential to
the operation of the company.

Without this instrument the brothers had
no quorum. She stuffed her fateful leverage in
a floppy canvas bag and walked. It was
a comic scene—the bulging bag, the swish
of her alluring skirt, sunglasses much
too big for any thief. The glamour served
to mock her legal crime as bling. At home
she filled a roll-on with cosmetics, a picture
of her parents, lingerie, her laptop,
and not much more. She left a note that she
was going home to Dallas for a visit,
"Your groundless jealousy belittles me."

She backed her Jaguar out and left that life
before eleven. Four years of marriage down
the tubes—the garden club, the lunches, and
drab afternoons of chick lit at her book club—
the heavy weight of Menelaus on her.
Behind her she left nothing. Did she feel
regret or shame, remorse or even grief?
Let's say that passion swept her forward so that
these questions never entered consciousness,
as if she'd left one frat boy for another.
Too bad for him, but he'll get over it.
Yet still a twinge of sadness stayed with her—
good girls did not betray their husbands. Did
an unseen moral stripe lay buried to freight
her leaving with an existential guilt?
Was her self-serving action in service to
her deepest Self? And how is this decided?

Was Menelaus to blame for her departure?
Of course he was no model of a man,

but neither was he evil. Jealous was
another matter. Was Othello evil?
Where both betrayed by primal, limbic fears?

But Helen? Helen knew the fault was hers
at least in part. She chose the easy path
instead of facing problems in her life.
Someone as bright as she had many options:
she could have worked at Rice or U of H,
or volunteered at the Jung Center
like Cassie. A PhD was not beyond
her skills. Or just plain worked in marketing
or sales. Is boredom license to break a marriage?
To ask forgiveness might have been first choice.
Of course divorce was not an option now
that she and Alex were screwing with abandon.

So what to make of Helen and her spouse?
Is blame or judgment something we can render?
Are memes a help or only parquet flooring?
Ditto norms and mores, moral values.
Is neural circuitry a certainty?
Is there a choice but living in the story?

Her leaving made no sense to Menelaus—
which is the understatement of our tale.
That night he found the note and called her folks.
Her mother said they hadn't seen her and weren't
expecting her. He knew at once and called
her cell, "I'm deeply sorry. I was wrong,
so please come home. I know that I was out
of line. Can we not talk this through, my love?
Come home to me."

"Look, Menelaus, I'm not
returning now or ever. I was prisoner
to your life. I need to live, not die
of suffocation." She hung up on him.

Dumbstruck, the man stood deathly still then grabbed
a chair to keep his balance. Alone and pale,
he trembled and let out a piercing wail
as if he'd lost a child, stood statue still
again, regained his calm, then cursed her soul
for being born and took a golf club to
her vanity then called his brother Aga.
"She's gone, the bitch is gone. I talked to her . . .
perhaps she's at her lover's place."

Next day,
they traced her phone, not they, a techy nerd
in their employ, to an address on Sunset.
He used the net to find the owner's name. Surprise,
surprise. The pad belonged to studly Paris.
The truth sunk in at once—they had their man.

Yet Agamemnon counseled one more try,
"Before we go all out in this campaign—
you know I will, you have my word on that—
call her again and give her one last chance."

"Don't be an ass, you know I can't come home,
if that is what you call your mausoleum.
You lousy creep, call Madame Tussaud. Get her
to fashion me in wax. Then find a ho."
She blistered him beyond the necessary,
but then in love and hate who is to judge
our actions when they boil out of fissured
pits in our reptilian brains? This seething,
almost spinal reflex is blameless like

typhoons or hurricanes or lava flow
in one view and egregious in another.

"We need to implement a two-fold plan:
a broad attack on all Martillo ventures,
and next a blow against their leadership—
against the Hammer and his arrogance.
For that we need Achilles' iron fist.
Young Alex counts for nothing in this scheme.
Why kill the little pisher now or ever?
Dear Brother, we must shake the laden tree.
        "Go home and check to see what's been removed,
if anything, besides her clothes, cosmetics.
Take care to freeze your joint account and assets.
Make certain nothing's missing from the things
in your deposit box. She might have taken
securities or instruments for spite.
Tell me, and then we'll crank this baby up."

The Biker's first surmise—that he was in
the clear, home free—perhaps was premature.
The scene was viewed by derelicts—a pair
of them, well, not exactly viewed since dusk
had settled in and they were far away.
The vagrants, high on coke and weed, were sure
a biker threatened Mestor and his wife.
The rest was vague—as gauzy as a Rothko.
They did not mention sidecars, saw no bird
or crime. "My man, it smoldered," one had said.
That's all we know except the wind came up
and blew a line of snow away, and so
they were distracted, pissed in fact. They heard
the police were looking. On a lark they sang.

The word got round, and at Café Apollo
patrons buzzed, so Hector heard the news.
Apollo Fuente De la Luz warned him,
"Be cautious, prudent. You know how many bikes
there are in Houston? Jesus, they're bums on coke.
Get real. They didn't even see a sidecar.
If they had seen his parrot, they would have
said so since it's too juicy to leave out.
And Mestor, they didn't mention him by name.
They couldn't tell your brother Mestor from . . .
King Achashverosh." A puzzled look. "Don't ask.
Perhaps Achilles is your man, but cool it.
I am disposed to help—I'll tell you when.
Then only question him. No threats or muscle.
Just try to tease out what he knows and doesn't."

Apollo, Hector reckoned, was a force
of nature. He had the pulse of Montrose.
Better listen. His knowledge was uncanny.
He drew a bead on rumors and conched the city—
all Texas—as well as any gossip maven.
Not much went on in any circle that did
not find its way to this shrewd Argentine.
When young, he'd fled his country's dirty war
and came to Houston with a wealth of contacts
both here and there—musicians, artists, poets,
doctors. His vision seemed oracular.
It's better not to cross him, Hector thought.
A great canoodle in Achilles' bed
propelled the lovers to think of drinks and dinner,
and soon the Hammer and the Biker would
be at Café Apollo locking horns.
So sated, high on love and pot, contented,

Briseis smiled: "First I have a joke
you'll never get. Should I tell it?"
    "Do it. Do it," Patroclus cawed and whistled.
    Achilles nodded.
                    "What did the Norwegian
fisherman aver as he proposed?"
    "You know that I don't know, so out with it."

"If you live by the fjord,
you die by the fjord."

"So bad, Briseis. I wish I'd thought of it.
Bad puns are very sexy—I want to poke
your ribs and somewhere else again as well."
    "First, let's go for spanakopita."
    The two came in, sat at a corner table,
and ordered drinks. At once the Hammer spotted him,
began to simmer, then boiled to a frenzy.
(Distracted, Apollo lost track of molten Hector.)
The Hammer was a testy piece of work:
The ex-marine had bivouacked logos on
his biceps—*fuerte* sprawled across the left,
while *suerte* volleyed back god Ares' nod.
    He glared then flared as he came up behind
Achilles and blurted out his caged-up rage,
"I've got a gun. I'd kill you here and now,
but that's too good for you. You killed my brother."
    Achilles kept his cool, leapt up, and turned
to face the Hammer: "I'd start with something civil,
my friend, perhaps, 'Hello' or 'Nice to see you.'"
    "Asshole, you better put a lid on it.
Come clean. Own up, you bastard. Two guys are sure
they saw a bike and biker in the park
the night that Mestor died, his wife went missing."

Achilles had had about enough of Hector,
"Which park, which night, which bike, what crime. What bullshit.
Unless there's something more you have to say,
I'm asking you politely. Leave, please leave,
I don't know anything about his death—
you're way off base with this. Once more, please leave."
　　Although the Hammer had a gun with him,
he wasn't sure that he could win a fight,
not even on Apollo's turf that night.
So Hector paused and glowered, flipped a bird,
and left, but not before he said, "I'll dice
you into cubes too small for fish to find.
Expect no quarter when I come after you."
　　"You couldn't dice a bowl of Jell-O, tough guy."
The Hammer skulked away. Achilles thought,
The Rolex, oh well, it's first class loot but lost.
I can't sell it. I've got to dump the thing.
　　"Earth to Achilles, come in," Briseis said.
He smiled at her: "He's mourning Mestor, that's all,
and casting for a target to discharge
his grief and maybe to exact revenge.
Relax. The music's good, so chill with me."
　　It's not recorded what Briseis thought,
or if she thought at all, but sure as sparks
when knives are held against a grinding wheel,
a clutch of neurons fired deep within—
and never surfaced to her consciousness.
What memory trace was left we cannot say.
As for Achilles, he thought to call his friend,
gray-eyed Athena Sapienza—for now
he could not do without her piercing counsel.

"She fucked us over, Aga, that bitch Helen,"
is what he caught from Menelaus' rant.

"Her jewels, our cash, and, most important, stock,
her voting stock, are gone. We cannot call
a meeting of the board without her. That brat
she's with, the pretty boy on Kirby, dead meat
is what he is."
                    Then Aga laid it out,
a careful plan, "Tell Hector and El Rey
that war's declared, the boychick must return
the vixen with the cash and voting stock.
If not, we'll scuttle all Martillo ventures.
A full assault's the only way to go."

              They'd buy the beauty shop and turn him out.
They wouldn't put a contract out on him,
not yet. The restaurants, who financed them?
Who owned the other buildings or were they leased?
La Migra could be used—undocumenteds
must swarm like flies in all their taquerias.
Might Agenor help to swindle them—
all men have a price and what was his?
The rumor mill suggests they laundered money,
perhaps sold drugs or even girls. Was there
a way to get at them through Mexico?
Or scandal? Surely, someone had slept with someone
or stolen something, did drugs or crossed some line.
This caper would be harder: In River Oaks
they were unknown; some digging was required.
Young Alex was the only one with ties.
Who Hector was, his weaknesses and vices,
his secret cravings were as foreign as
the ebb and flow of tides off Zanzibar.

The stalwart brothers struck with pen not sword—
a letter went to Hector and his father
and threatened legal action: Alex abducted

Helen and helped her steal their stock and assets
was the claim—a lawyer's letter, a bluff,
that much was plain. It was a lame tirade,
less than the dribble of an old man's pee.

The word was out on Helen. Someone tweeted:

> She loves Paris in the springtime,
> she loves Paris in her fall.
> This Paris is her lusty bloke—
> she doesn't feel the cuckold's poke.

The buzz was everywhere—downtown, the clubs,
the Galleria. People spoke of her
with awe as if she'd broken out of prison.
The cuckold found huge lipsticked horns across
his windshield and Hersey's kisses on his hood.

Sweet Helen was fucking her studly lover Alex.
The world was fucking over Menelaus.
The brothers were in trouble, big time trouble.
They needed Achilles out in front on this,
so Aga called the Biker, made the ask:
"I'm calling for your help to set things right.
My brother's lost his wife, I'm up shit's creek.
She took her stock and stole my voting stock.
We need a quorum to run the company.
What say you to a little friendly help?"
　　　He'd seen the way that Aga ogled B.
Was coveting another's woman "friendly"?
No love was lost between the two of them,
but Hector's crudeness at Café Apollo—
his in-your-face insistence that Achilles
killed his brother Mestor sealed the deal.

(As if he were an innocent accused!)
 He paused a second for effect and said,
"I'm in. I'll rattle Hector's cage but good.
He needs to eat a little humble pie,
which I'll serve up to him with all the fixings."

As for the macho brief the brothers sent,
surprise, surprise, the family laughed it off.
Old Priam worried,
                    but Hector said, "There is
no substance to it. They are blowing smoke"—
which made the buy-in of Achilles crucial.

Sort through the story's shards for moral right
in vain: Achilles, Menelaus, Alex,
Aga—their rapes and murders, lusts, and loves
and tenderness. The human soul is blind,
a tiny grub translucent in the darkness.
The story's all we have, and not as guide.
Don't hazard bets on what the goddess plans,
for if you sleep in Aphrodite's bed,
instead of love you'll wake to find your balls
in Dite's ferret mouth. And in disgust
she'll spit them out like so much putrid silage.

BOOK VI. THE BIKER AND THE BIRD

ARGUMENT. Achilles arrives home one evening to find Patroclus disconsolate with jealously. Briseis has left her black lingerie on their bed and Patroclus is attacking it. Achilles calms him and recognizes that the bird's raging may be valuable in the future. Briseis returns from BrioBrio and also reassures Patroclus that she loves him. The focus shifts to Agamemnon, who suggests a planning meeting at Achilles' house. He and Menelaus attend along with Ajax Gross, Ajax Kurtz, Odysseus, Nestor, and Idomeneus— as well as Achilles, Briseis, and Patroclus. Agamemnon again ogles Briseis, and after Odysseus tries to warm up the audience with a joke at the expense of the Martillos, Agamemnon lays out the plan he rehearsed with Menelaus: The brothers will target Martillo interests, and Achilles will accost Hector. Achilles seeks the counsel of the Athena within. Initially she excoriates him for killing Mestor and suggests contrition and atonement before she will help. He asks her to understand his weaknesses, and she tells him to begin with deeds: Deal with Hector to secure Helen's return but use wit not force. Achilles' plan involves retraining Patroclus to rage at a white bra and panties. They visit Hector at his office where Achilles humiliates and intimidates him. After an initial confrontation, Achilles throws the undergarments in Hector's face, and Patroclus flares up and gashes his shoulder and ear drawing blood. The encounter ends with an enraged Hector swearing to kill Patroclus. Athena expresses her anger at Achilles' mishandling of the visit—he should have thrown the lingerie on the desk.

Achilles found Patroclus in a snit—
disconsolate, he cocked his head and hissed,
a mix of cobra spit and raptor rage,
directed toward the open bedroom door.
"My God, what's wrong? You know that daddy loves you.
Tell me, lovely Bird, what's eating you?
I've never seen you so upset. Please stop."

      He picked him up and kissed him on the nape
then held the struggling white macaw to him.
He tried to soothe the bird. The flailing stopped,
but only when he took him to the porch
and paced and rocked him like an infant son.
Inside, the bird broke loose. He swooped, and strafed
Briseis' bra and panties on the bed.
He clawed at them and spewed a limbic rage—
flung like a Chinese throwing star.

                                  "Patroclus,
you're jealous of Briseis, the love we have.
My God, I don't believe what's going on.
I've got a jealous lover on my hands.
No, baby, I have love enough for two."

      He grabbed Patroclus, held him close again,
and closed the bedroom door to hid the trigger.
Who could have guessed my Bird would act this way?
I'll tell Briseis to put her lace away.

      At once it clicked. "There's value here, Patroclus,
if we can harness your engrained behavior.
Let's work on this unwieldy gift together."
Smart bird, my Bird, but, boy, is he a handful.

      Briseis walked in fresh from BrioBrio.
"What's wrong, my love, you look distraught and sad,
as if the world's about to end? Tell me."

      "Brace yourself. Patroclus is mad jealous—
he's jealous of our love. Can you believe it?

He vented feral hatred of your lace:
he flew at it as if we're out of place.
He's jealous like it's going out of style."
                    "Oh, dear, Patroclus. Stop. I love you too."
She scooped him up and held him to her breast.
"I love you almost as much as Big Guy here.
Trust me, Patroclus, to me you're very special.
I hold you like no other in my heart."

The loss of Helen, voting stock, and shame
welled up and festered, an angry carbuncle,
that poisoned every thought of Menelaus
and his testy brother Agamemnon.
Enraged, the brother took the lead, suggested
they hold a summit at Achilles' place
to rally friends and win support for action.
                    Next night the guests who gathered at the Biker's
where greeted by his T-shirt's cheeky boast:
"Atlas Shrugs, Achilles Acts" in black
was blazoned on his muscled chest and back.
A feisty Agamemnon and his brother—
tight-lipped, red-whiskered, horny Menelaus—
hosted friends, conspirators and partisans.
Big Ajax teetered on a folding chair
too small to fit his frame—or frame of mind.
And Ajax Kurtz with wrestler's build and agile
sat cross-legged, impatient on the floor.
Briseis, always gracious to a fault,
set out a lavish deli spread for all.
Lech Aga held her in his lusty gaze
as she bent over braless with a tray.
Nearby Odysseus caught Aga out,
but worse, the Biker saw his throbbing leer
and wary laid it by to even scores.

Without the Mensa T-shirt he deserved,
retired Professor Nestor Gibbon came,
and even discreet Idomeneus arrived
to show support. All thought the man aloof,
indifferent to the straits of Menelaus.
Unslaked, lay hidden his yearning for adventure.

"Before you get things going, Aga, I have
a little quiz," Odysseus began.
"How many Martillos does it take to screw?"
        "If you don't mind, I'll just lay out the plan."
He listed all the options in detail
and summarized his talk with Menelaus—
the squeeze on Alex' shop if they could buy
the building, the Martillo restaurants,
illegal workers, pressure on Agenor,
his thoughts about their money laundering.
Next came the threatening letter they had sent.
"We haven't heard back yet. My guess is that,
like us—if we got such a letter—they
ignored the sucker. It was worth a shot."
        But how to pressure the return of Helen,
their voting stock and hers by heat on Hector?
The issue was not Martillo businesses—,
the brothers thought that they could handle that.
For Hector, something more was needed. Gross
suggested Alex, "The cocky guy's the key.
Hit him, and Helen will be back in minutes."
        "Young Alex is a brat, too soft to count
as a combatant, and Priam's old, too old,
so that leaves my man Hector," said Achilles.
He glanced at Aga, whose face confirmed their talk
was off the record. "Look, I'll deal with him."
        Around the room relief was palpable.

Yes, let Achilles secure the wayward Helen.
Whatever it took with Hector he'd prevail.
    "I'll figure how to shake him up," he said.
"I don't know what I'll do, but it will come
to me. I'll scare him, rough him up a bit,
no more. We don't want any police involved.
I'll think it through and then get back to you."
    Off the hook, their spirits high, by turns
they praised Achilles for his leadership.
Patroclus whistled, secure and happy for him.
Little did the Bird of Paradise
suspect his part or price in waging war.

Just how was he to forge a measured strike
against the Hammer—one both bold and velvet?
From deep within he sought Athena out,
she, who by dint of effort, Fate or luck,
and careful husbandry might help him now,
but only if he faced his darker side.
    He called Athena, his demanding muse,
his childhood friend, the girl from dancing class,
the valedictorian who went to Yale,
the polymath, his confidant, the love
he dared not love, the girl who chose the route
of loners, who loved this man as part of him.
    Athena from the first declared herself
untouchable and settled in with him.
Achilles acquiesced: Her terms were chastity,
autonomy, and always the last word.
Her presence was so finely atomized
he could no longer separate her out.
    She lived in Houston now and ran a small
boutique consulting firm but really lived
inside Achilles' soul or skull or psyche—

the naming's not important. She dwelt within,
inside his being so that inviting her
to lunch was lunch alone. Alone with her.

A presence in his presence, she ignored
directions and pressed on with her agenda—
"You call on me as commissure of journeys.
What can I, your mentor, do but listen?
Great sympathy is what I feel for you,
but murder? Never. Though I reside in you,
I can't abide your brutal rape and murders.
For sport alone you killed two innocents.
And now you ask my help. You are unworthy.
I am your you, or part of you at least.
The greater you is held accountable.
The judge is you or should be you—your Self.
If not, forget me. You need another you."

"Athena, that's not what's on my mind right now."

"I'll be the judge of what is on your mind.
You kill a guy and want to plan a prank.
I'll help, but only if you get a grip."

"Just name your price? What do you want from me?"

"It's simple really. What do you want from yourself?
Contrition and atonement are a start."

"I don't know how to set things right with you.
It's not a formula like math. It is
a calculus of incongruent goals.
Cut me some slack—I'm just a man, that's all."

"You miss the point completely. You're not a man.
Try deeds, not words. So let's begin
with how to handle Hector face-to-face:
Meet him and take Patroclus, no knives or guns.
Make him return the girl with wit, not force.
Meet me half way on this. Be wise and calm.

The rest can wait until you pass this test."
She vanished like a spider in the wind.
Her threads remained and glistened in the sun.

As guileful as that spider, he spun his silk.
He went to Marshalls, purchased bras and panties,
and kept them under cover in a bag—
cheap whites, imperfects, but invaluable.
    "Patroclus, I need your help, I sorely do.
We are going cruising for Martillos,
but first I have to train you for your task.
You know Briseis loves you, finds you sexy,
and yet your jealousy got out of hand.
The bras and panties are an object lesson.
We'll do some classical conditioning
and switch one trigger for another. Not
exactly Pavlov, but don't worry."
                        And bit
by bit he trained the bird off lacy black
brassieres and panties that Briseis wore
and onto Marshalls whites. The rage remained,
the flaring wings, the shrieks, the falcon pose
but now directed at new undergarments.
He was, Achilles joked, "A martial bird."
Patroclus, fierce and ready as a raptor.

He called the Hammer's office for a meeting.
Next day, he primed Patroclus. As agreed,
he left his armor home. In riding leathers,
black ones . . . try to imagine a wealthy guy
from River Oaks and MIT, who lived
in Montrose, killed a guy and raped a woman,
who harbors muse Athena in his psyche,

in black leathers on a weathered bike
with sidecar and a bra-crazed white macaw.

Too much? Okay, breathe and we'll go on.

Martillo Ventures officed out on Hillcroft.
In strode the paladin with white Patroclus
on his shoulder and a Marshalls bag.
The duty cop was reading *Field and Stream*.
He nodded as if a rider in black leathers
who sported a white macaw was usual.
        "The girl inside can help you find your party."
        He asked the *chica* at the desk for Hector—
not necessary, the office doors were open.
Old Priam occupied the largest and
was on the phone, *"Por supuesto que sí. . . ."*
Some others were reserved for Alex, Cassie,
Mestor and their sibs—he guessed they all
drew pay. And there was Hector's next to Priam's.

Rouge Hector was sarcastic and direct.
"What brings you here, *patrón*, a search for nachos?
Slumming are you? Montrose, River Oaks
are where you hang. So out with it, you scum.
You came to fess up over Mestor's death . . .
you chicken shit. You are their errand boy.
They want to ransom Helen, I'm sure of it."
        "I give you credit, you are almost right.
I told you I know nothing of your brother.
But Helen's gambit gnaws her husband's innards,
and Agamemnon festers over stock.
His brother's loss of Helen makes him seethe,
so they'll not quit till they've had satisfaction.
The deal is this as far as you're concerned:

we all demand her back along with stock
and cash and any other things they stole.
And note that I say 'we.' We hold your brother
Alex led her on, seduced the woman—
by taking up with her, encouraged her.
We offer nothing. We demand her back,
or . . ."

What? You'll kill the lot of us—and Priam?
Fat chance, I'm not afraid of you, *patrón*.
What else, friendo? . . . Nothing? . . . We're done. So out."

"We'll see." Achilles reached into the bag
and tossed the bra and panties in his face.
"You pussy, try these on for size. Do it."

"Do it. Do it," Patroclus shrieked and flew
at Hector's face. He thrashed about but missed
the bird. A claw tore through his shoulder.

"Puta,
you mother fucking bird, I'll have your ass."

"Enough, Patroclus, stop!" No luck. Achilles
had neglected an off-switch in his training.
The bird strafed Hector's head and lanced an ear—
bright blood. Achilles grabbed the bird, held on,
then hooded him, recovered, paused, and spoke,
"So, friendo, we want safe passage back for Helen."
The Hammer held a hanky to his ear.
"It stands between you and your piece of mind—
and Priam's, the stud's, and your entire clan's.
Just send her back with all attendant loot.
If not, it's war—your clan against us all.
No way that you can win this fight, I promise."

"Get out, you cunt, *pendejo*, out of here.
I swear to you I'll butcher him, that bird.
You'll rue the day you brought your parrot here.
So scram. If you touch us, you go to jail.

I kill a bird and then what? Avicide?
No one ever died in Huntsville charged
with avicide. Get out, *pendejo*, out."
    "You touch Patroclus, and I'll kill you myself.
You'll be so dead the worms won't find your body.
They'll be nothing left to putrefy.
Return his wife, the property, it's over."
    "We haven't even talked about my brother.
You'll pay for Mestor and his wife, I swear—
and swear that you'll regret you fucked with me."

Athena pulled no punches with Achilles—
tongue-lashed the arrogant adventurer.
"The Hammer's right, '*pendejo*' does the job.
To call you 'moron' is much too kind for you.
You ask for counsel, we talk, but you're obtuse.
You could have managed this without the blood . . .
by tossing bra and panties on the desk.
What's wrong with you? Your mother is a goddess.
You're proof the gods give birth to nincompoops.
You have no call for your display of wrath.
Your acts have sown a cycle of vendetta.
You haven't heard the last of this from Hector."

BOOK VII. DESERTION AND ABDUCTION

ARGUMENT. Poseidon conspires with Aphrodite to sow mischief, the end result of which is events that enrage Achilles and bring him into conflict with Agamemnon. The god causes a storm to damage Agamemnon's garage apartment where his girlfriend Chryseis lives. All her clothing and personal effects are ruined, and she moves into his house to a bedroom near his. She discovers he is having simultaneous affairs but dismisses these as dalliances. To win him back she visits Aphrodite at Boutique Cythera to buy sexy lingerie. Aphrodite hints that she has sold similar articles to at least one of Agamemnon's conquests. Chryseis is incensed by this further conformation of his infidelity and decides to go on a shopping spree, pack up, and return to her hometown of San Angelo. She thinks of herself as a Christian woman with standards who has been wronged, unlike Helen who in her view is a tart. With Chryseis gone, Agamemnon concocts a story to cover her embarrassing desertion. He has always been obsessed with Briseis and decides, whatever the cost, he must have her as his live in. Menelaus warns that Achilles is unpredictable and will retaliate. Agamemnon sends Eurybates with a friend and Dr. Machaon, his physician, to BrioBrio where they intercept her in the parking lot, drug her, and deliver her to the garage apartment that has been refitted as a prison. As the book ends, it is clear that Menelaus was right: Achilles will bring Agamemnon to accounts over Briseis' abduction.

Poseidon savored mischief at least as much
as Aphrodite and joined her in a plan
to slam Chryseis who'd betrayed tart Helen.
So he let loose a storm of schmutz-filled rain
and stalled the tempest over River Oaks—
the gods delight in trickster schemes like this.
It undercut Achilles with its force
and swept away all claims of moral high ground
the preacher's randy daughter might assert.

Recall Chryseis lived in the garage
apartment as Agamemnon's chattel, ho,
and servant and in the view of heaven had
no grounds to judge fair Helen's escapades.
In retribution the god unroofed her place
and set disgrace astir with gale force winds.
The tiles stripped, the wallboard ripped,
a sheeting rain arrived with gutter sludge,
debris and grit, and loathsome creepy crawlies.
Roaches, fledglings, mice, and slugs were lofted,
and everything soaked through and ruined. For starters—
the bedding, cushions, chairs and clothes (sweaters,
slacks and dresses, underwear), and shoes,
cosmetics, contacts. Chryseis' girly stuff
was a colossal mess.
                    Now, in his house,
ensconced nearby his bedroom, she lived too close.
She saw his treacheries in living color.
At first she set aside the evidence.
It's just a fling, a stage that he'll pass through.
It was a fateful, grave miscalculation:
rich Agamemnon had a string of girls
that he could take or leave, but mostly took.

Yet always in the background was Briseis,
the Biker's girl, and his outsized desire.
Pent-up, unvented, his need glowed poker-hot.

Naive Chryseis thought to win him back
with thongs and tiny bras that flattered her
ripe wares—a *schmatta* cannot rouse desire,
so off the rack was not a useful thought.
The shops in River Oaks and Highland Village
would not do—she needed drop-dead chic.
But where to find exotic, sexy gear?

Some dumbass neurons raised Boutique Cythera
and shopping spree that blemished Helen's mien.
If she had only known what misery
she'd reap at Dite's hand, she never would
have gone. The goddess would destroy the snitch.
Thus, devilish Aphrodite, not to be
outdone, soon struck her like bubonic plague.
The seamstress and brassiere designer knew
the how of sewing discord in her bras.

Chryseis entered cheerily and put aside
Briseis and the yellow cardigan.
"I've come in search of your discretion," she said—
as if the two were longtime confidants—
"to talk about the rain and ruined clothes."
She could not know that god and goddess were
designers of her woes. Next she complained
that Agamemnon's fire seemed to bank.
Did Dite have ideas to ensnare him—
not ready-to-wear but something über chic?
      "Would you believe you're not the first to ask?"

Then Aphrodite murmured sotto voce,
"A certain lady, well-endowed and not
in need of my support, came in and begged
me for my help. . . . I can't divulge the rest."

"Go on. I need to know. Please, out with it."

"I shouldn't talk about the lady or what
she bought and can't reveal my client's name
or his. You know the parties well enough."

"That shit. You mean another woman has
her talons into him, some men's club floozy?"

"Chryseis, that's you're surmise. I didn't say that."

"You might as well have spelled it out in red.
This man's been cheating on me left and right.
She's not the only one who's screwing him.
How many, Dite, how many have you helped?"

"There's nothing I can say, my lips are sealed.
I'd be out of business if I talked.
Let's say the market's brisk for trade like this.
You know men swivel at every swishing skirt
that happens by, and Aga's no exception.
It's best to bow out gracefully, Chryseis.
Go home, Forget this life. Trust me. Go home."

The live-in, hot purveyor of pussy said,
"The ingrate. I helped that man in every way.
I found out Helen, exposed her tryst with Alex.
He seemed so charmed by me and captivated.
I can't believe I'm out. I won't beg him.
Unlike that whore, I'm saved, a Christian girl.
I have myself to live with. I'm principled.
I'm not some girl he can pick clean of flesh,
discard as if I were a tart or hussy.
I'm out of here as quick as I can manage.
I knew he dallied, but this thing hit me hard.
What a rotten motherfucker he is.

I thought the man would marry me someday.
I don't know how to thank you, Aphrodite."
        "Don't mention it." She really meant her words.

So true, he won't remember how she helped
with Helen and his brother's thorny problem.
The man was loyal as a greasy film.
For her devotion—her total focus on him—
he had the memory of a pubic louse,
the kindness of a jackal. He was spineless
as a squid. He'd find another pretty doxy
to be her warm-bed proxy.
                        Screw you, Aga,
I'll find another wealthier than you.

Was it Moline, Aurora, Urbana, Mobile,
Sedalia, Longview, Cuero or Sequin?
Or maybe Tulsa, Norman or La Grange?
What town called back her beautiful used body?
Was it the Baptists, Methodists, or Church
of Christ who welcomed her to fellowship
in her father's church? We just don't know,
so let's move on. Before she left, she used
his credit card to buy a slew of clothes
replacing her trashed stuff and adding more.
When Aga was on business in New York,
she stuffed her girl loot in a Vuitton bag—
her diamond studs and brooches, a ruby ring,
an emerald watch, and pearls. She placed this gloss,
her spree, and suitcase in her pricy coupe,
and then she split—disposed of by the gods
like useless glitter dross or something faux—
angelic, blameless toward San Angelo.

Well, macho Agamemnon had a fit—
raged like a cornered pit bull. Her leaving screwed him.
He didn't care about the jewels or money.
If word got out that his kept mistress scrammed,
his friends would smirk. His enemies would gloat.
The slightest chink in his facade was death—
a mortal blow—for that was all he had.
"Hey, Agamemnon, getting any nookie?"
"You've lost your touch, you wreck of a lechless lech."

You know where this is going: To be held up
to ridicule was ugly. No fate was worse than shame.
(Remember snake brain had no sense of guilt.
Entitlement was all he knew, his due.
Take all. Take what is given and what is not.)
He needed lightning action to save face,
and so he had a line if word got out,
"Chryseis went to see her ailing father.
I talked to her last night. The girl is fine."

Now Agamemnon huddled at his club
with Menelaus. Both ordered single malts
and waved away the menus. Aga flared.
His eyes exploded with a livid anger
that could find no worthy target save
Chryseis. He was hot as solar plasma,
"Goddamn that stupid ho, I'll wring her neck."
To make his point, he torqued his napkin tight.
"Goddamn that bitch. You give such girls the moon—
uncouth, small town lookers, no more than hookers,
whose only future life is on their backs,
and look at them: They leave without a note.
The coupe, the diamond studs, and credit card—
I canceled it—you can't buy gas with pride.

She's in San Angelo. I've traced her phone,
or rather our tech guy traced her phone out there.
I told him not to cancel it. I'll pay
and gladly track that bitch's sorry path.
Slut goddess got her in her sights for sure.
People get in tizzies and get stuck,
do dumb ass things. It won't end well for her.
She's mired in a dismal Texas town.
My sweet, enjoy your father's righteous church—
the socials, prayers, and Sunday bible study.
        "Enough. . . . I have a problem, brother, so tell
me what you think. I can't go on pretending
Chryseis will return. I'll say her father's
about to die, that she's an only child,
and so on. Easy enough. So here's the thing:
I want another live-in, someone special,
not any spa-toned body, but a beauty
as fair as Farah Fawcett or Jane Fonda
in their primes. In fact there is someone
I hanker after. You know the woman well.
No secret, it's Briseis, Achilles' bobble,
the plaything he extracted from a bar,
and now I want that diamond for myself.
I think of her in bed with me . . . and, well. . . .
The Biker is a megaproblem, a giant
mother-fucking headache, but I'm sure
I can prevail with money and some cunning—
unless some nasty quirk of Fate directs
events and fucks me over royally.
At any cost I have to have that girl."

His appetite was Casanova big:
the need of randy hinds for harts in heat
or tomcats for their mollies paled compared

to his. A billy goat was juiceless, spent,
and lions lacked cojones, ditto stallions.
     Her beauty gnawed at his good sense. Her charm
was not her warmth or wit, her kindness, love
of fun or graciousness—only her face
and body, which could be displayed in public
and other men would envy. And the thrill
of taking her from arrogant Achilles
aroused the pleasure centers of his brain.
     "Now tell me what you think." He pounded the table
so hard the room turned toward him. People stared
as if to say, Take it outside, you doofus.
"My friends, I'm sorry. I apologize.
Go back to your libations, enjoy the evening.
Again, I'm sorry I disturbed your drinks."
And to his brother, "You'll see. I'll make this work."

Volcanic Menelaus was surprising
as he spoke: "Best not to go there, brother.
We need him on our side. The rogue's a wild card.
If he deserts our cause . . . scratch that. If you
abduct the girl, which must be what you're thinking,
Achilles will come after you and kill you.
The rumor is he killed that Mestor guy.
Trust me, the utmost caution is in order,
or you could pay a price so brutal you'll long
for death—Scorpio and Dirty Harry
will seem as light as Stewart and Colbert.
To have him for an enemy is peril.
Think hard if this is what you want to do.
She's not the only pretty girl in Houston."
     "Put a lid on it. I have to have her."

So here is how it went, this crazy notion:
Pursued by lust and blinded by desire

and shame at the desertion of Chryseis,
he hatched a plan shot through with faults and doomed,
a clotted monster born of Ares' spawn
with Dite that clouded his sensorium
and thrust him into injudicious action
flailing like a sailor in a bar.
Make no mistake, his was riff-raff thinking
from a man in Ferragamo ties.
All men are riff-raff in the face of sex.
Add war and it's disaster. Ask Mussolini,
Napoleon, FDR or JFK.
Think LBJ or Ike (we all liked Ike—
wife Mamie, voters and Kay Summersby).

First Aga put a crew to work to fix
Chryseis' place—debris was hauled away.
Besides new carpet, drapes and paint, a roof
and metal doors, he bought a king-size bed
and sheets and towels. Security was added:
window stops affixed with one-way screws,
and keypads, cameras, and special locks.

Next he prevailed upon Eurybates
to go to BrioBrio with a friend,
extract the girl, and bring her home unharmed.
How to abduct her from a public place?
To Agamemnon's credit, the plan was deft,
ingenious really, and involved Machaon,
his doctor, who could bring his expertise.
        "Remain outside. Please don't go in the club.
The boys can snatch her near her car," said Aga.
"And don't forget your drugs. They're critical."
        Athena could have quashed the ballsy foray,
but stayed aloof for reasons she held close.
        Surprisingly it went without a hitch.

They waited by the car. Soon unsuspecting,
she approached. They grabbed and gagged the trophy
while Doctor M. injected Demerol.
She fought a moment, but soft as summer fog
Machaon's ether cone relaxed Briseis.
Their captive stretched out in a panel truck,
the doctor with her in the back, one drove.
The other followed closely in her car.
In twenty minutes she was in his keep:
she lay in bed, attended by Machaon,
drugged and locked down tighter than San Quentin.
Achilles' other bird was in her cage—
the doors and windows sealed, first-rate surveillance,
no phone or laptop, scissors, knives or razors.

How now Briseis? Dark prince Aga owns you,
and River Oaks is not where people look
for those abducted. You are like a Greek
antiquity removed without permission—
for now he cannot show you anywhere.
Just how to cast you into bragging rights
is Aga's problem—and thus is yours as well.
Without exposure who can trace you here?
At least in Hell the devil knows one's where-
abouts. Bad break, Briseis, really bad.

Intent and will are useless sans the gods,
and all save one ignored her plight for now—
there's too much sport in watching her distress.
But random chance soon roused a counter force,
and Tyche summoned help on her behalf.
Did Aga really think that he could hide her
the way that Castro hid the girls in Cleveland?
Would wise Athena allow this sacrilege?

So she befuddled Aga, enshrouded all,
the gods included, in cloudy self-delusion.
Dear reader, relax, for help is on the way:
Bold Tyche brings her mettle to the fore—
Achilles settles this ignoble score.

BOOK VIII. HIGH CRIMES AND MISDEMEANORS

ARGUMENT. When Briseis fails to return from BrioBrio, a worried Achilles calls the club and then visits Café Apollo and tries her cell phone. No one has seen her. After a sleepless night, he learns from Odysseus that Agamemnon has abducted her. He asks him to get word back to her that he will rescue her as soon as he can. Achilles recruits Hector's unwitting help in harassing Agamemnon and Menelaus by spray-painting a message on his office door demanding Helen back. Thinking the message is from Menelaus, Hector calls his Mexican cousins and gets them to pressure Pemex, the Mexican Oil giant, to cancel a contract with the brothers. Then Achilles enlists Pentha and her gang of Amazons to spray-paint the brothers' cars with "HELEN STAYS." Before the brothers can respond, Hector forces a shutdown of their Baytown cracking plant and causes the near collapse of their waste disposal company. Under Apollo's spell, Hector suggests an implausible solution: a fight between Alex and Menelaus to settle the fate of Helen and her voting stock. It ends in a draw. Faced with mounting financial losses, the brothers swallow their pride and offer to return Briseis and a million dollars cash if Achilles will help with Helen's return and the cessation of Hector's sabotage. Achilles insults Agamemnon's manhood and counterdemands the return of Briseis, five million dollars, and a seat on the company's executive committee. In anger Agamemnon changes the deal: He will keep Briseis but offers the higher sum and the seat. Surprisingly Achilles accepts. With the money and the seat safe in hand along with the help of his mother Thetis and Poseidon, he rescues Briseis.

Briseis isn't back. It's two a.m.
By now she should have texted, called, or come,
he thought. He called the club. At BrioBrio
they said she'd gone. She'd left alone at twelve.
"As normal as dental floss" was how one girl
described the night. He asked about her car,
and she went out to look. "No, it's also gone.
I'll let you know if she comes back or calls."
On impulse he stopped by Café Apollo.
She wasn't there and hadn't been that night.
        And then, befuddled, he did the obvious.
He called her mobile phone then texted. Nothing.
In fact the tone was odd. *It's not working.*
He found Patroclus' gaze as if to say,
She's in trouble, Bird. We've got a problem.
He did not call the police. *Too soon*, he thought.
He had no evidence that harm had come
to her yet knew that something wasn't right.
She wouldn't disappear at night without a call.
They never went to bed without the sense
the other was okay. He was distraught.
"Patroclus, something's very wrong. I'm worried.
My love has vanished like mist before the sun."
And so the Biker passed a sleepless night.

He was beside himself when Odysseus
came round to share a "rumor" that he'd heard.
(His friend Eurybates had spilled the beans):
"I know you're in a state about Briseis.
For now she's safe, unharmed, but Aga has her."
Achilles tried to speak. . . .
                        "Hold on a sec.
So here's the story as best as I can tell.

It's ugly, brace yourself. Here's what happened."
    "What happened! This is utter bullshit. I'll . . ."
    "Just once shut up and listen. Aga sent
three guys to BrioBrio where they drugged her.
They kidnapped her and brought her back unconscious."
    Achilles' neck veins bulged. He sprung up fuming.
    "Jesus Christ, sit down and let me finish.
They've stowed her where Chryseis used to live.
Remember the garret over his garage?
My source says she's okay. Nothing's happened."
    "I should have guessed. I'll kill that rotten bastard.
I need her back. I'll worry till she's safe."
    "She's locked down tight—confined to solitary.
Agamemnon is obsessed with her.
You can't talk reason to him. He thinks of her
as compensation for Chryseis' loss.
The man is crazy as a rutting moose."
    Achilles, always volatile, now blew.
Mount St. Helens seemed a simple flare.
"The rotten SOB will pay for this.
He's got no claim on her but appetite.
It's lust and arrogance that's driving him—
he's always held the world was his to take.
I'll fix the bastard. He'll fold when I play hardball.
No way he'll get away with this, you'll see.
I'll cut his nuts and feed them to my Bird.
But first, Briseis. I need her safe return.
I'd call the police, but that's too good for him.
The man must beg for mercy and his life.
If he's so much as laid a finger on her,
I'll scar his face with my initials. Tell him
I know. And leave the rest to me.
I'll fix that cur the way a vet would fix him.

Get her a message: Explain I know that Aga
has her and tell her to relax, be cool . . .
and not to fret, that it will take some time."

Achilles chose his plan with craft and guile
beginning with diversions to distract
the thief. That night he gathered Bird and tools,
drove past Martillo headquarters, and sprayed
the doors and windows—"I demand her back,
you fuckers. Helen is my wife"—in blood
red letters. Confident, he cooled his heels—
he knew the shark would rise and snap the bait.

Yes, Hector's fuse was ultra short. He called
his kin in Monterrey and had them talk
to giant Pemex Oil, who pronto sent
an email canceling the brothers' contract.
Like David's shot, the Hammer brought Goliath
to his knees.
    What was Achilles' thought?
Cat-fast, the Biker fired another salvo.
Ex-boxer Ares (a friend of Hector's) was
his friend as well. He had a daughter, Pentha.
Whip-smart, she led a gang of teenage girls
and took delight in mirthful interventions.
  "I have a favor—could your daughter's gang,
the Amazons I think they're called,
be hired for some undercover work?"
  The Biker dressed them like a football team
in black and scarlet jerseys, helmets, facemasks
and slyly sent them through the parking lot.
They found the brothers' twin Mercedes, sprayed
the windows black, and lettered "HELEN STAYS"
across the doors. For fun they keyed the cars

and set off the alarms. Closed circuit caught
the girls. Security informed the police:
the vandals were a pack of high school boys
and noted that the color's matched St. John's.
    St. John's? No matter? Agamemnon knew
that Hector sent the truants—this style was not
Achilles'—and swore revenge. He called the office
and asked to speak to Hector. Curse words streamed
from Agamemnon's mouth. He ended with
a threat: "You cut the crap or you'll be dead
or begging to be dead," and then hung up.

No way that this could threaten him. This time
the cat-like speed was Hector's. He moved before
the brothers knew what hit them and targeted
a Baytown cracking plant they owned: A fire
broke out. It hurt the brother's pride more than
disrupting operations. Hector, somehow—
it's not exactly clear—had cut the power
and forced a shutdown of the place. The taunt
was Hector's, they surmised, but they had no
response. (Achilles gloated, but more important,
unlike the brothers still in disarray,
he had a plan to take Briseis back.)
    Still on a roll, the Hammer telephoned
Agenor to enlist the broker's help.
Smug Agamemnon and his brother had
positions in some local stocks, small deals
in Houston companies. One was a waste
disposal venture that spread collected sludge
on private property. Agenor called
some favors in. With help from savvy friends
he planted claims on blogs and message boards
that EPA was canceling the permits.

The business counterclaimed at once, but who
would not be nervous? Would anyone believe
these owners with a vested interest? The stock
nose-dived. Although no one could find the source,
the rumors were now truth. The brothers boiled.

So there it sat: the Hammer hammering,
Achilles, the Avenger, agitating,
the brother's paralyzed, Briseis caged.
The Bird of Paradise ate less and less.
Still fat cat Agamemnon had not approached
his morsel in the cage Chryseis fled,
and Aga, horny as he was, knew not
to touch his captive. Without Achilles' help
they were marooned, resourceless, south of nowhere.

That night with calvados they cursed the Hammer.
They had a plan, but as we know, the task
depended mostly on Achilles. The hype
about the rents and leases, illegal workers
required finesse to implement, and they
could not deliver. They languished. Even bragging
about the girl was out. He had not tamed
the filly and could not trot her round the ring.
Checkmate. He was afraid to touch his prize.
Checkmate. He was afraid to show her off.
Checkmate. Menelaus remained dishonored.
        Achilles was the answer to their prayers,
but who could think the Biker would respond
with anything but vengeance? They must have known
Achilles knew they had the girl. How could
these master strategists think otherwise?

Achilles, engineer from MIT,
the Biker and Avenger with his muse

Athena and Patroclus, without Briseis.
They had no choice but him, who was no choice
at all. A haughty pride and lust were driving
Agamemnon on a different course.
To stop the scourge of Hector's ire, he schemed
to hire thugs to kidnap Alex and hold
the man until the family surrendered
both Helen and the stock and pledged an end
to violence between them.
                              Before they could
take action, Apollo seized the Hammer's mind.
Unwitting envoy, Hector sent an email:
"Let's settle scores the manly way. Café
Apollo's neutral turf. The two of them,
our feuding brothers, let them duke it out,
the winner to take all—the bride and booty."
        Improbable in Montrose? No, not really.
Far stranger things have happened there. A fight
would do the trick. Why injure dozens when
a brawl might curb the rage and quell the wrath?
Some honest, good old-fashioned fisticuffs
to tamp the fires down. Imagine this:
one night, a dapper stylist—a dandy—
sashays in to meet a portly red beard
in cargo pants, a crimson fleece, and boots.
(If you can picture this, you'll understand
why savvy moguls cast Brad Pitt in *Troy*.)

So here is how the main event played out:
delicious slapstick, tasty *wunder* shtick,
a mix of Buster Keeton and pro wrestling.
At last the red beard sat astride young Alex
and banged his head against the floor till it
was bloodied. Quickly Apollo Fuente moved
to separate the two, declare a draw.

Both sides erupted and loudly cursed Apollo.
      "You've had your bread and circus. The bar is closed."

The dust up left the issue unresolved.
The brothers crawled back to Achilles, what
else could they do? With Pemex down the tubes,
the crippled plant in Baytown, waste disposal
in the toilet, they had to cut their losses.
But how to bring the hussy and her stock
back to the fold? They had to eat some crow—
Hector, the Hammer, was beating them to death.
That made their sole recourse the Biker's mettle.
      The brothers acquiesced. They knuckled under,
and fear trumped lust. So Agamemnon tapped
Big Ajax, the trusted college friend, sage Phoenix,
the man was like an uncle to Achilles,
and wily Odysseus, instructed them
to strike a deal: Achilles would retrieve
the stock and Helen. In return the lech
would send Briseis home untouched and throw
in cash, a million smackeroos as redress.
                                    The Biker
didn't miss a beat, "You know I want
his nuts."
            "Look, cut the shit," Odysseus
retorted. "Of course you're pissed at him. I get it,
but cool your jets and listen. I think he'll move
and ante up a million more. What say?"
      "I say, 'Fuck off.' He cannot steal my love
and go scot-free. Tell him I'll fucking break
his kneecaps when I see him."
                                    Ajax Gross
chimed in, "Remember math at MIT?
You know, not all equations have solutions.
What did he tell us, Randerath? Remember?

You have to set aside the ones that don't
and focus on what works or nothing gets
designed or built. Achilles, name your price.
I'll make it work. Put honor, anger, pride
aside. Your goal—Briseis safe and sound—
comes first. Get done what can be done, my friend."
    "I hate to say it, but you're right. I want
Briseis back. Patroclus wants her back."
    He spread his wings and whistled, "Do it."
                                          "Tell Aga
that he's a piece of shit. Go on a bit,
just make the insults up. So here's the deal—
Briseis home, unharmed, five million cash,
and most important: voting stock, a seat
on the executive committee. He never
should be free of what he did. Tell him
his only other choice is strangulation,
with compliments, of course. Go tell him that."
    A smirk? Contentment? Orgiastic peace?
They could not read his face. Perhaps all three.

That night the three returned. Odysseus
told him that stubborn Agamemnon balked.
"The cash was fine as was the seat you want. . . .
After I relayed your sentiments—
I softened them—he cursed you to the heavens.
A look came over him. He nixed the deal.
'Tell him I've changed my mind, Briseis stays.
And screw the cops, the world, and fuck Achilles.'
He's dug his heels in, she is off the table."
    Like Kasparov, Achilles had a plan,
"Tell him okay, that I accept his terms.
I want a check that's certified, a letter
too by noon tomorrow or it's off."
    Odysseus and Ajax seemed surprised,

could not believe his choice. "You sure, Achilles?
You want to think this through? My God, Briseis."
    "It's over, done. Just tell him what I said."
    Phoenix, remembering the strong-willed boy
Achilles was, could not be taken in,
"We'll pass this on, of course." His wrinkled face
was Bobby Fisher to his Kasparov.
"Okay, Achilles, I'm sure he'll go for that.
We're done, my friend, unless there's something more."
    Achilles shook his head, "Bring home the deal."

The Biker showed them out and closed the door,
then turned and saw Patroclus, head beneath
his wing. "No, Bird, don't worry. She'll be back.
The brothers, both of them, will drop their guards—
they cannot see beyond their fear and lust.
Odysseus is shrewd, and Phoenix knows
my gambit mode is stealth. They sense the guile
and will recount the offer—not betray
my thoughts, so Aga will think that he has bought
my loyalty, that I'll secure their Helen,
that each will have his chattel in this bed,
that meddling Hector's gone or even dead."
    He kissed Patroclus on his nape and smiled.
Achilles sighed and whistled softly. Patroclus
whistled back and fanned his raptor wings.
"I have a plan to free Briseis, but first
I want the check to clear, the voting seat
to be delivered free of strings. I'll act
when this is done."
                    Next day, they both arrived.

Midafternoon he chatted with Patroclus:
"I'm headed home to seek my mother's counsel.
It's always wise when I'm in need of help."

The Biker's mother Thetis owned a spread
in River Oaks not far from Agamemnon,
but most important, she'd be keen to help.
    "I'm very glad that you came by to chat.
Come sit out by the fountain and let's talk.
Sit there in that wicker chair and spill
the beans. What's going on? I've heard a rumor
that you and Aga are going at each other.
My neighbor's not a bad sort, just spoiled rich.
Your mother wants to know what's up? Come clean."
    "Your so-called neighbor kidnapped my Briseis.
He's holding her in his garage apartment.
I'd seen him eyeing her but didn't think
the sleazy creep would act on fantasy.
The scumbag snatched her from a parking lot
and thinks to keep her under house arrest.
The man's a stupid motherfucking cunt."
    "Don't speak that way around your mother."
                                        "Sorry."
    "You make it sound as if I've raised you poorly."
    "I'm up to here. I love that woman—she
subdues my demons. I have to have her back.
He's got her in his private keep, so it's
your help I seek to get her out unharmed."
    "Seems Aphrodite took a bite of you."
    "For sure. But now let's focus. Here's the deal.
I'll change from jeans to khakis and a shirt,
then walk to Aga's, jump the fence, run up
the drive, take down the guards, and bring her out.
I'll need your help. Just wait in your Mercedes,
and when I flash my light, drive up and we'll
hop in."
        Poseidon listened while they talked
and heard his plight. *The boy can use
my help*, he thought. So as Achilles walked,

the Brawler, Squaller, and Fountain God sent sheets
of rain in front of him and followed it
with thunder claps. A bolt of lightning struck
the captor's mansion, putting out the power.
Another strike disabled the transformer.
The hits set off alarms, which caught the guards'
attention and distracted them the more.

A cheetah leap, then up the drive. He grabbed
and choked one guard and motioned to the other
with his tire iron, "Go up and get
the girl. One word and fatso's dead. And drop
your phone. Now move!"

Briseis was confused.
The rain obscured her view, but then she heard
Achilles' voice, relaxed, and let the guard in.

"Don't call the police unless you want me back,"
he warned the guards. The Trident God assured
a lasting outage to cover their retreat.
He took her hand as they raced down the drive
then forced the slaver's gate. Now on the street,
he flashed a light. Quick Thetis caught the sight
and moved. In minutes they were safe at home,
at ease, and chatting in his mother's kitchen.
Achilles' boyhood room was home to them
that night—the lovers in a single bed.

Next day Briseis made Achilles laugh,
"A single bed is fine. A single toothbrush—crazy.
A Boy Scout toothbrush too! Imagine my
Achilles as a Boy Scout in a tent."

Later Thetis dropped them off in Montrose.

BOOK IX. *THE ILIAD* AND THE ALAMO

ARGUMENT. Nestor Gibbon is invited by the Jung Center to present a public lecture on a subject of his choice. Off the top of his head he suggests *"The Iliad* and The Alamo," but as the date approaches, he realizes the comparison is spurious and decides focus on the Alamo. The audience is filled with all kinds of people drawn by the intriguing title, though Achilles and Hector are missing. As planned, Nestor veers from the topic and discusses the Alamo almost exclusively. He traces the cruelty of the Mexicans back to the Moors who brought savagery from North Africa to Iberia where it became an important staple of Spanish life. Cortés spread the tradition to Mexico, and Nestor claims it colored Mexican rule in Texas and Santa Anna's campaign there. The Texians, as the early Texans were known, used this brutality to justify their rebellion, when in fact it was really about escaping from Mexico's prohibition of slavery and Mexican taxes. In short, according to Nestor, the Texians were nothing more than opportunists. During the talk all kinds of people make objections. Nestor brushes these aside. He is resolute in claiming Texans are not critical enough of themselves or their past. Texans tend to glorify Texas and fail to recognize their shadows and own their shortcomings. His conclusion rankles the audience. When someone asks about the relation between Troy and the Alamo, he says that there is no specific relation, but cruelty has been and always will be a part of human character. "Man is wolf to man," he quotes and adds that, even worse, man is man to man. Odysseus dismisses part of Nestor's argument but praises his overall conclusions.

The Jung Center is famous for its courses,
so when Professor Nestor Gibbon proposed
The Iliad and Alamo as topic
for a special lecture, he drew a crowd
across the gamut, as if all Houston came.
The Center was a neutral meeting place.
By custom you checked your baggage at the door—
you were supposed to anyway. Let's see.

Odysseus was there, prepared for nuggets
Nestor might dispense like pearls before
the crowd and diamond chards to undercut
their hubris—let's put that aside for now.
Both Ajax Gross and Ajax Kurtz arrived.
Idomeneus had come and Phoenix too.
Apollo, Helen, Alex, sister Cassie—
a Center volunteer—sat patiently.
Aphrodite hid, secluded in the back,
while Agamemnon and his brother were
up front, perhaps to lend complete support.
A.E. and Henrietta Markham showed.
As we shall see, it's even money if
Athena was disguised as Henrietta.
And lawyers, some politicos, a judge,
and teachers, Rice professors, therapists—
Paul Dillinghaus for one—an architect,
some business and financial types as well.
Bill Morgan, the construction magnet, came,
and Tuffy, too, his wife, to hear the talk.
Fred Schneider, Nestor's friend, flew in for it.
Achilles' mother Thetis and Machaon,
the doctor, showed, though not the Biker or
his Birds, nor Hector, but old Priam sat
respectfully. Get this, amazing: Ares

and daughter Pentha sat together. Who knew
the teenage leader of the Amazons
was Harvard-bound that fall and ripe for all?
The house was packed with peas from different pods,
and all awaited Nestor's erudition.

It had begun some months ago. He got
a call. The Center wanted him to speak
about a subject of his choosing—something
attention-getting Sean Fitzpatrick said.
        "How bout the Alamo and *Iliad?*'
I think the topic of the Alamo,
an *Iliad* redux has real appeal."
        "Sounds great, but don't say 'redux' in the title.
You're bound to lose attendees right and left."
        "Okay, *The Iliad* and Alamo."
        "I like the sound of that. So it's a lock
unless I hear from you," Fitzpatrick said.
"Send me a J-peg photo and an abstract."

        But as the time approached, he had regrets.
The title had appeal, pizzazz, not substance.
*I can't go through with this. The heroes of
the Alamo aren't mythic heroes in
the sense of Homer's characters. A hero . . .*
his thought trailed off. Could he equate the siege
of Troy with Santa Anna's? He was in trouble.
Achilles, Ajax and Patroclus were
apart from mortal men. And Travis, Crockett,
Bowie, who were they? No, what were they?
He didn't want to go there. Then he did.
He thought of Joseph Campbell. *If the hero
had a thousand faces, which was the face
of those who fought for Texas at the mission?*

Almost with delight he set aside
The Iliad. He thought this gave him license
to discuss a favorite peeve, how Texans
inflated Texas. Well, he had no license.
He'd speak his mind and take the consequences.
    So going forward Nestor had a plan—
not to show the ways of God to man,
but to destroy the hubris of his city.
The talk was quite devoid of Troy and Homer.
We cannot capture all of what was said—
so here's a modest reconstruction:

"Good evening, friends, and thanks for turning out,"
Professor Gibbon said. "I have to limit
tonight's remarks, but let me preface them:
Our Houston is a motley blend of grit
from eighteen thirty-six, the wildcat mind,
the rebel South's unyielding code of honor.
That's not to say that Asians, Blacks, Latinos
play no role, but still the culture's Anglo.
By rights I should begin with hoary Troy,
but Texans always find the Alamo
compelling ground for self-examination.
So in accordance I've revised the order:
the Alamo is so engrained it smolders
in every schoolboy's heart, corrodes our views,
distorts our values . . ."
              "Crap, pure crap,"
a suit stood up and said. "Have you a whit
of sense, Professor? . . ."
             "Let me flesh this out,
and then you'll have a chance to speak. And so
we have a vaulted view that holds ourselves unique.

The Alamo and Lone Star represent
a complicated legacy that's mixed.
Our self-reliance, common values, faith,
tenacity and grit we should be proud
to keep. But what about our shadows—Vidor,
Jim Crow, our nonwhite poor, a safety net
in tatters, arrogance, and fear of failure—
and success—our guilt, our fear of being shamed?
Should we today be proud of those things too?
Or Stanford Capital and Enron? Surely
their comportment's far removed from ours.
You think these crises could have happened anywhere. I have a very different view."

  The business types sat sullen, staring at
their shoes, tight-lipped or even snarling. Did they
expect a night of heroes? Others seemed
more open or at least less hostile. Unsure
his message would get through, he paused and looked
around engaging them and smiling, "Friends,
tonight we'll set aside fierce Montezuma
since everywhere the Amerindians
were cruel and jettison our myths as well—
the Texas Rangers and Comanches. Their roles
were minor in this drama.

       "Now I'd like
to focus on the Moors, their legacy.
They sealed the fate of Texas." He caught the eye
of Dillinghaus who seemed to nod approval,
but others squirmed and looked back at the door.

  "Professor, what's this got to do with us
or Homer? Montezuma, I don't believe it."

  "Let me develop this and flesh it out.
Moors swept across the straits and into Spain—

then called Al-Ándalus—and brought a code—
a mix of tribal harshness, moral absolutes,
and justice shorn of mercy—that took hold,

not as the law, but as example to
the local people who mimicked Berber rule.
This residue remained in Christian Spain.
It stained the Spanish view of Moors and Jews,
including Ferdinand and Isabella's,
and underpinned the Catholic Inquisition.
The monarchs of Castile and Aragon
shipped code and venom west. For us tonight
the key's Cortés, who slaughtered all at whim.
With time in Mexico this code had morphed
and burrowed deep within the skin of all—
aristocrats and *campesinos.* So
when Santa Anna spared no man at Béxar
and Goliad, he played a potentate
who might have been a zealous Moorish Berber."
        A hand went up. "Professor, I'm confused.
Tell us what this has to do with Texas."
        "Well, Santa Anna," Professor Gibbon said,
"was party to prevailing attitudes
and killed and tortured many captives and
thereby legitimized the grievances
of Texians, who really had no claim at all.
They hated Mexican control and taxes.
Texians said they fought for liberty—
self-serving rhetoric, hypocrisy.
As part of liberty they planned to bring
in southern slaves to work their fields and stock.
So much for our nobility of spirit.
Black slavery would fuel their enterprise,
and 'wanton' Mexico forbade all forms.

So slavery, free land, and taxes spurred
rebellion without a thought of compromise.
It was a land grab made to look heroic."

A colleague interrupted, "The Greeks were not
so noble. Victors took the men as slaves
and girls for chattel. Why hold them up as models?"
"You have a point. They're flawed like all of us.
Their motives shadow us, and that's the problem.
We've made a myth of Travis, Bowie, Crockett,
who I believe were the most flawed of men.
I know it's hard to take, but here's the point:
this Santa Anna was a friend to Texas—
his harsh suppression provided an excuse
for all we planned before he headed north
and used to justify what Travis fought for.

"Today it's easy to ignore our slaves
and grifters, speculators, and our treatment
of the Indians. Were we so pure?
Of course we were. After independence,
Juan Seguín was used to sanitize
the Anglos' sordid treatment of Latinos.
Call it what you like, but we behaved
like victors everywhere. We're not immune.
We're human. We have our warts and shadows. So when
Sam Houston declared the rights of man at stake
at San Jacinto, he was right—but not
the way that he implied. He claimed defeat
of inhumanity and victory
for freedom, our Bill of Rights reconsecrated.
Amigos, he was wrong about the rights.
The rights the Texans brought were slavery
and freedom from the greater good, a right
that gave no credence to the other. Yes,

we learned from Santa Anna and reaped rewards
by improvising on our southern past.
Make no mistake that is our legacy."

"That's not our legacy at all. You have
distorted everything that Texas is,"
a man held forth. "Your talk is travesty."

"It's not at all. It takes a balanced view.
Like you I'm proud of Texas, but stop and think:
Not everything we did was just or fair."

Soon hateful looks began to overtake
a restless segment of the crowd. Athena
sat cooped up in Henrietta Markham
and thought to let him take the heat alone.

"I have a final thought before the break:
The worst of the Old Testament and Koran
first marched across the Rio Bravo then passed
the claim of moral high ground to our rabble.
In truth that is our common provenance.
I'll take some questions now or we can break."

A lawyer in the back held forth about
the State of Texas, its greatness and importance
for our nation. "Don't you think, Professor,
that Texans were essential to our claim
beyond the Sabine, in fact to California?
Without the Alamo and Goliad
so little in this region would be ours."

"Pure nonsense," Nestor said. "The Yankees would
have taken it. Jackson or perhaps
Van Buren, Tyler, Polk. They were rapacious—
a hunger justified by Manifest
Destiny, prosperity driven
by a code that sanctioned cheap slave labor.
So much for the Southern view of honor.

Eventually, one way or another
they would have owned it—by crass
maneuvers, stealth or war or subterfuge.
The States had money, numbers, Yankee knowhow.
The seat of Mexico lay far away,
a thousand miles south. They foundered,
spent by a war with Spain just newly over.
A campesino from Oaxaca had
no interest in land beyond the desert,
no reason to march north except conscription.
William Barrett Travis notwithstanding,
our Houston by some other name would be
here—as American as war and rape.
Forgive me if I dramatize to make
a point, but Texas is not unique or special.
Our Texas, though I love it, likes to view
its own importance much too highly. Some days
I think it's nothing but hot air and hype.
I'm sorry for the tirade, but I'm tired
of self-important Lone Star Texas. Your thoughts?"

A young blond woman who resembled Helen,
perhaps was Helen, said, "Professor Gibbon,
I spent a year digging out a tell
at Troy. What is your argument? How are
the Alamo and Trojan War related?"
        "Good question. After break we'll come to this.
But briefly there is no allegory here,
for Troy is not the Alamo or Rome
or Waterloo or Dunkirk, not anyplace
but Troy. And Santa Anna's not Achilles
or Agamemnon in ancient Asia Minor—
though ruthlessness and wrath, offended honor
played a role in each. And decency

still quivers, bayoneted in a ditch.
We should expect no more—chimpanzees live
this life. We share their DNA. The question
is progress. Is there any human progress,
or must we live forever with our darkness?
Where are the 'Better Angels of our Natures'?"

Most people were dissatisfied with his
remarks. His onslaught seemed a bait and switch,
that Troy was not in any way his topic.
Was Nestor's plan to bring *The Iliad*
to life in service to his arguments
about the Alamo? It's hard to see
his logic or design. Perhaps he thought
for men at sea each tale's a harbor beacon
that lights the path to discipline and honor.
More likely he wanted to imply how far
in Texas we have fallen from the Greeks.
It might have been the baseness of all men—
self-interest effaces every prospect
of the hero's life—he sought to capture.
Was his a condescending ploy to geld
opponents before they spoke? Let's listen to
attendees thoughts about his canny rant.

The audience was buzzing: "A little hard
on us." "I don't think he gets it." "The man
is out of touch with modern Texas." "I
am on the board at Rice. It's liberal crap,
such talk. I'll have his name expunged."

                                    Not all—

Odysseus to Ajax: "Vintage Nestor,
the kind of thing that no one wants to hear."
        And Aphrodite eyed her flame, buff Ares,
as if to say, These yahoos have no *sechel*.

Whatever Aga or his brother thought
they held their tongues. Nestor was a friend.

Before the speaker could resume, a hand
went up. It was attached to perfumed money,
"Professor Gibbon, would you care to say
a word about Crimea?"
                              "Why Crimea?"
          "I'm curious to hear your take on strife
and ethnic tensions. Are there lessons there?"
        Our designated hitter had been lobbed
a softball, "Sure, but just a brief digression.
Crimea is our child."
                        The room became
so still you could have heard an ant break wind.
"They're Russian speakers on the far edge of
Ukraine with strong allegiance to the east
and other ethnic Russians. Push came to shove,
and they declared an independent state."
        "But why are they our child, Professor Gibbon?"
        "We English speakers lived in Mexico,
as a minority far from the country's
hub, close to our fellow English speakers.
We broke away to serve our goals and greed,
or maybe out of fear or God knows what.
When we declared our independence, then joined
the Union as a state, we countenanced
that path for others. Crimean rebels are
true Texans. They are doing what we did."
        "So what about the War Between the States?"
        "Perhaps another time. We must move on,"
and Nestor turned to his prepared remarks.

We won't recount the second half—it was
a quick-paced digest of the Trojan War—

except to add one pithy observation.
Before the evening ended Nestor said,
"A devastating human truth from Plautus":

> *Homo homini lupus est*
> Man is wolf to man.

"The saying is correct but incomplete—
Man *is* wolf to man. Nothing new
in that. But man is also man to man,
and there's the sadness, tragedy and pity.
Nothing will change that we are Cain and Abel."

As people left, the host complained about
the talk—the second half did nothing to
redeem bold Nestor's views or tactics.
Disagreement reigned—a handful thought
he got it right; for most the Alamo
and Goliad were cheapened by his take.
        One well-dressed man remarked, "Professor Gibbon's
nuts. We own this land. Forget Troy
We won our rights with blood."
                            Another said,
"I don't see the point. The Mexicans
were out to screw us over."
                        Cassie wanted
to chime in about the future, but
decided for the present not to speak.
        Paul Dillinghaus was put in mind of Jung.
He liked the talk and found it balanced and
just right, the proper mix of light and shadow.
He knew it worked because it rankled many.
        Bill Morgan said to Tuffy, "Gibbon
might have a cogent argument about

secession, but there's nothing to be done.
We can't hand Texas back to Mexico,
nor should we. History is written by
the victors but lived by all of us. My point:
People living ordinary lives
for decades dull the cutting edge of ancient
claims, compel us to regard the here-
and-now and privilege it above all else.
I don't quite get Professor Gibbon's point.
Why be contentious and inflame us all?
His self-important judgments rankle me.
You know what else? He's smug, the guy is smug.
    But Tuffy didn't buy his line of thought,
"Smug, my love—that doesn't make him wrong."

Odysseus now drove the oldsters home—
both Phoenix and proud Nestor sorely wearied.
    He spoke in courtesy to Nestor, "Do
you really believe the bleakness you expressed?
Deep down, I mean. Is life so unrelenting?"
    "Well, if you want the good news Bible or
the Promise Keepers, you need to talk to someone else. Just look, my friend, at history.
Remember how it ended for your namesake.
After Troy he wandered ten log years,
got home and left again. Forgive the jest,
but life's a journey—for you, for me, for all
of us. We are no more than wandering Jews."
    "So is it true for you, this Troy, I mean?"
    "The question's wrong. But Auschwitz? AIDS? Or think
of Gettysburg. Or Bernie Madoff. I'll
skip over hantavirus, global warming,
despoiling of the planet, depression, cleft palate,
the rape and murder of innocents, extinction.

The Darter, Pileated Woodpecker
and Ridley Sea Turtle are bound for Dodo land.
And veal, foie gras, Chilean sea bass—all these
in theory are avoidable. Should one
take a life to save two lives? Trade-off—
always unfair—is everywhere. My friend,
you'd have to drive to Skagway, not the Heights,
for you to hear it all. And always there is
darkness. The business of living is a mess.
Even Sinatra didn't have it his way.
My friend, go home to your dog, your wife, your son."

At home, Odysseus, the ever wily,
was sure the lecture made no sense: The link
between the savage Moors and Mexico
was clear, but not the spindly thread that stitched
this harshness to the early Texans' actions.
Nestor was remiss in leaving out
The Iliad's stark view of rage and duty.
His friend was tactless too in dressing down
the crowd with his unsparing diatribe.
Yet Nestor got it right to flag our firm
avoidance of our deepest fears and shadows.
Whatever Nestor's faults, Odysseus
admired the good professor's erudition,
if not his logic. He also loved his heart.

BOOK X. AJAX GROSS AND AJAX KURTZ

ARGUMENT. We find out more about Achilles' two close friends from college, Ajax Gross and Ajax Kurtz. Gross is driving with Kurtz and Odysseus to a Greek place for coffee and baklava. As he tries to park, Hector's red Camaro cuts him off, and the Hammer claims the parking spot. A fight develops. Tough as Hector is, he is no match for Gross. The two scuffle, and Gross picks up a brick and breaks Hector's mandible and maxilla. On his way to his café, Apollo drives by, sees the fight, stops, and with the help of Kurtz and Odysseus separates the two and saves Hector. As sirens approach, the three friends slip away to the Argo for dessert and more than a little ouzo.

Ajax Kurtz is obsessed with Cassandra whom he saw at Nestor's lecture at the Jung Center. Seized by raw carnality, Kurtz fantasizes about a evening alone with her. On impulse, he shows up at the Jung Center and finds Cassie at the reception desk. He tries unsuccessfully to take her to coffee. Cassie says that she can see the future and knows that he is motivated only by lust. Backed by Aphrodite, she dismisses him, but he vows to have her by force if she refuses his advances. Kurtz says that if she can see the future, she knows that he will take her and she might as well give in now. She tells him to get out, that she is calling 911.

A parking space, a simple parking space
set off a brawl that brought the Houston police.
Well, parking and a craving for baklava.
Ajax Gross had called Odysseus

along with buddy Ajax Kurtz. The three
were headed for dessert and idle chitchat.
The driver, Gross, had eyed a spot on Montrose.
The trouble started when the Hammer's red
Camaro skidded to a stop and blocked him.

     Nail-hard and sculpted, Gross was six-foot-six,
all muscle, with the darting movements of
the swallowtail that bears his name. The man
could scour macadam using Hector's face
and brighten his to boot. Oh, *pobre* Hector.
The other two were seasoned, street-smart savvy,
and rivals when it came to fighting rumbles.

     The Hammer was an ex-marine with service
in Iraq. His brawling, ugly streak
might pass for courage. Really, though, it was
an inborn, limbic reflex, raw and sharpened
to an attack-and-kill response, embedded
and free of any cognitive intent.
His grit was pure Komodo dragon courage—
one lacking all finesse and nuanced judgment.
But still we should not diss the Hammer based
on neuroscience: Hardened, bold, he served
his country well, unstintingly. The man
was tough enough to lead marine platoons.

He leaned against the hood of his Camaro
and taunted Ajax, who sprang out and eyed
him up and down—his Tony Lama boots,
his belt with silver buckle, black jeans, tan shirt,
and cowboy hat. "Excuse me, but I was
about to park here."

              "My man, I got here first.
You want to park? I'd try the lot across
the street."

"Better listen, cowboy. I was
the first one here."
"You pussy, park across the street."
Out came the boys and stood behind big Ajax:
"My friend, I think it's time for you to move
your car. We're looking for dessert and not
a butchered cowboy. Before there's trouble, move
the wheels."
The Hammer: "Move them? You want this space,
you come and take it."

At once the two were at
each other. Hector charged and lodged a shoulder
in the pit of Ajax' stomach, lifting
him. Then Gross reached down and poked beneath
his xiphoid. Hector winced and, crushed by Ajax'
weight, precessed and landed badly on
a knee, then crumbled. Now up, he lunged and tried
to gouge out Ajax' eyes. But as he reached
across, his armpit was unguarded, and
big Ajax pressed so hard he palsied Hector's
axillary nerve. The Hammer shrieked.
Weak-kneed and faint, he wobbled but somehow kicked
the big man in the groin. He groaned and cursed
the Hammer's mother and his sisters. Both on
their feet, they circled looking for a breach.
Then testy Hector charged and took him down.
On top, he smartly pummeled Ajax' face
and bloodied knuckles as he landed blows
on Ajax' nose and mouth and bruised
an eye. Big Ajax rolled him off and stood,
then grabbed a brick, and broke the Hammer's jaw
and maxillary arch. Half-crazed, contorted,
the Hammer moaned in pain but found the strength,

to slam the man against a wall. Swift Ajax
jabbed him in the nose, then crossed and sent
him reeling, raised him up, and dashed him to
the curb.

      By chance, Apollo, Hector's mentor
(dare we call him that?), was driving by
to his café and saw the brawling men.
He stopped and froze the action. Fuente got
between the two. Odysseus and Kurtz
restrained Big Ajax while Apollo cradled
Hector.

      "You two are worse than common thugs.
I can't believe it—neither of you has
a whit of sense," Apollo fumed. "You're dumb
as stones, no more than snarling curs. It's not
the dirty war, the streets of Buenos Aires,
or Pinochet's unsparing purge. You're here
in Houston—get a grip and call it quits."

      They heard the sirens blocks away and left
the sullied Hammer in Apollo's arms.
Big Ajax and his friends still planned dessert
although a change of venue was in order.
He chose another Greek café, the Argo,
that offered baklava and ouzo—lots
of it in eight ounce tumblers for a song.
They drank and drank and drank, got loud, and sang:

      "Ouzooo something to me
      something that simply mystifies me."

Let's turn to errant Ajax Kurtz, whose heart
of darkness was as bleak as Conrad's sump.
His groin sent wiry Kurtz bestirring urges.
It started at the lecture Nestor gave

when he caught sight of Priam's wayward daughter—
Cassandra, lovely, warm, inviting, seated
across the row and fetching in a jumper
that emphasized her form.
      Who is that girl?
I have to have that beauty—now, he thought.
These urges occupied his thoughts each day
at NASA. At night they overwhelmed his sleep.
This hunger hardly was unique to Kurtz—
the others in our story shared his . . . what?
It's imprecisely called by many names.
Let's look a bit more closely at this "what."

These men, these hormone-driven bulls, were all
alike—Agamemnon, Menelaus,
Odysseus, Achilles, Gross and Kurtz.
Testosterone can summon fire so fierce
its blaze consumes all decency and judgment,
its lava swamps ambition, purpose, drive.
  The six, including Kurtz, were educated,
had loving mothers, sometimes wives and sisters,
but when stiff Eros grabbed them by the scruff,
they were as singular as rutting moose.
The common good was routed from their ken,
as Eros primed the pump of lust in these
determined men.

      Now back to Kurtz who spied
a stranger in a room and fell in . . . love,
desire, lust, or craving, want, or need.
No single word will do. It puts us to
the test: Our love and lust are minted like
a coin, placed in our palm heads up or down
by Fate that presses us to spend its heat.

So Kurtz imagines Cassie—a fantasy—
alluring Cassie, blond hair loose, enticing,
and sitting with him in a quiet bar
enjoying a Manhattan. Fingers touch.
She coos and smiles coyly, flicks her tongue,
exhales and licks her lips. She's seen this in
the movies. Then she purrs and reaches out
to him, and he picks up a swizzle stick
and strokes her arm—a promissory note.
She takes the stick, runs it along his cheek.
By now his fantasy consumes him.
They laugh. He signals for another drink,
again to share. His scripted beats go on.
They look into each other's eyes, in truth,
see nothing but imagined bliss and fire.
So totally caught up is Kurtz, he thinks
they cling to one another desperately
and yearn as if belonging were a given.

He never thinks his reptile brain could be
in league with hormones driving the bolero
of their infatuation. They order fresh
Manhattans with an extra dash of bitters.
But nothing seems to matter. They are touching
beneath the table, stroking, coping feels,
and groping, being groped. Soon they head back
to her apartment, turn on the lights, and turn
them off, take off their clothing, kiss and fondle.
The tender love they make feels fresh and young,
unsullied by pot or coke or even booze.
His skin against young skin—against her skin.

His fantasy continues, heaven sent
it seems. The real world never enters in—
the sordid world of clubs and drugs and one
night stands. Next morning, they don't ask about

the night before or why they are together
or how they picked each other, where, or why
they failed to use protection, or why they can't
recall the names of their eternal loves.

  They get up, pee, pop back to bed, push up
against each other—hard—without regrets
or hesitation. They are happy now—
he summons brilliant moonlight and Vivaldi—
are happy naked in each other's arms.

  He's getting off on this and loving it.
It works—that is, the magic of this little
passion play this evening as he moons
about Cassandra whom he does not know
but thinks he loves with all his heart. Cassandra,
conjured object of his dreams, young Cassie,
the fully feminine who will complete
the person that he wants to be, the lily,
Cassandra, construct of his fantasy,
no more, but no less either. The receding
muse that he cannot embrace, refuse—
the anima that grips him from his slough.

If only he'd restrained himself, not acted,
let well enough alone, had clarity
to trash the lust brought on by neural demons
—that chthonic, soul-poised plague of Marburg virus.

  He acted out his fantasy: One day
as Cassie met Jung Center visitors
and regulars up front, he spied his dream.
She sat bewitching in a white silk blouse—
supported by an Aphrodite bra—
and at her throat a single strand of pearls,
redoubling her enchantment, so she glowed
a warmth so winning Kurtz was smitten—resmitten—

for he was smitten from his first encounter
at Nestor's lecture weeks ago.
                              He said,
foregoing introductions, pleasantries—
as if he'd known her twenty years or more—
"Cassandra, I predict a future for us."
        "That's dangerous with me. I know too much."
        "No, I predict I'll get to know you well."
        "Depends on how you parse the verb to know."
    This calculus amused the engineer:
"A little glib, so let me try again.
I looked at you the night that Nestor talked
about the Alamo and thought, I want
to get to know her. So I asked, and someone
recalled most days you work the front part-time.
I just came by to say 'Hello' and ask
you out for coffee after work today."

A longtime friend of Cassie's brother Alex,
the goddess would not abandon her to Kurtz.
So let's watch Dite help her parry him.
The goat came calling in his courting clothes—
gray slacks and tailored shirt—but prescient,
wise Cassie saw a gnarled Ratso Rizzo
whose steadfast goal was getting her to bed.
(Poor Kurtz, the Fates had doomed his enterprise.
Damn Aphrodite, Dustin Hoffman, those
online videos of *Midnight Cowboy*,
and his bad luck that gnarled Ratso Rizzo
was for her the true north of deceit.)

Tone deaf, he asked her out again for coffee
and got rebuffed a half a dozen times—
politely stonewalled. She said she was involved.

This sitcom starring Ratso Kurtz and Cassie
went on and on. When he was in one day,
a vagrant asked to use the restroom. Kurtz,
she thought, could be his brother. Again unfair,
but Aphrodite protects her own. They sparred,
now interrupted by the phone or people
looking for the bookstore or a course.
	She found him charmless as a welt and said,
"Please, Ajax, I'm not interested. I can't
be any plainer. Trust me, you should leave."
	"I not the man you think. Give me a chance
and come for coffee."
				"You are the man I think.
The course is clear to me: Your line will be
about the way I've captivated you,
my beauty, charm, and how well-spoken I
am. Then you'll say, 'I've never met a woman
like you. Your presence takes my breath away.'
You will go on about a quiet dinner,
and three dates in you'll want to screw. And then
you'll pledge to call and disappear like that."
She snapped her fingers, frowned, and turned away.
"I know these things. The future's clear to me."
	"You're wrong, dead wrong, give it a try. You'll see."
	"No, Ajax, I already see."
				"What's wrong
with you? You're so uncivil." His voice was shrill
and loud, almost a shout.
				"I've told you, Alex,
that I'm not interested. Uncivil? Not me.
Please leave before I have to summon help."
	The man from Mission Control now lost control,
"You bitch, you sniveling bitch. I'll have your pussy
one way or another. Better lock

your doors. And always look behind you when
you walk or jog alone. I swear I'll fuck
your brains out. Even if I have to kill you."

"Get out of here, you scum. If you don't leave,
my brother Hector will come after you."

"If you can see the future, get a grip.
You know I'll have your body now or later.
So chill, go with the flow."

                          "Get out of here,
you sicko. Now. I'm calling 911."

BOOK XI. CAFÉ APOLLO

ARGUMENT. Agamemnon invites some friends to a meeting to help plan an attack on Hector, whose strategies have continued to undermined the Atrides brothers' business interests and whose brother Alex and Helen have crippled the company by absconding with voting stock. He would also like to force the return of Helen to Menelaus. Besides the brothers, Ajax Gross, Ajax Kurtz, Odysseus, Nestor, Idomeneus, and Dr. Machaon attend. Still bristling over Agamemnon's abduction of Briseis, Achilles refuses to join them. Athena too withdraws her support and relaxes at a karaoke bar. Agamemnon suggests they show up at Café Apollo; eventually their presence will provoke a response from Hector. The plan works. Still recovering from his injuries at the hands of Ajax Gross, Hector and his friends arrive at the café. Apollo counsels him to be patient. Soon Apollo puts on deafening music, dims the lights, and sets Hector's side in motion. In the ensuring fight, Agamemnon and Odysseus are injured, and Aeneas punches Nestor. Poseidon intervenes with a thunderstorm which knocks out the outdoor lighting. Othryoneus, who is in town to woo Cassandra, corners Idomeneus behind a dumpster and slashes him. In self-defense, Idomeneus pulls a gun and shoots him. Hearing police sirens, Agamemnon's party slips away, not realizing that Idomeneus has shot Othryoneus. At first Hector is expansive about their victory, but when word arrives that Othryoneus has been killed, he swears revenge and selects Achilles as the easiest target. Athena, not realizing that she will be needed, continues to carouse at the karaoke bar.

"My friends," said Aga, "you know why I've asked
you here tonight. Martillo mania erodes
our enterprise, and Helen's loss remains
a wound disgracing Menelaus. Worse still,
our firm is paralyzed by voting stock
now in control of Helen and her lover.
I've got to force their hand and do it with
a show of strength before the Hammer bludgeons
us to death. He's driven spikes of chaos
into the heartwood of our company.
They listened: Ajax Gross and Ajax Kurtz,
the engineers, Odysseus, both wily
and combative, Idomeneus, the trusted
wild card, the boiling cuckold Menelaus,
the internist Machaon, and Nestor too.
They hung on every word: Some had a lot
to lose—Odysseus and Ajax chiefly
who owned stock.
                    Absent was enraged Achilles.
When he returned the call from Aga, his
response was blunt, "You guys can go to hell.
You would have kept Briseis for yourself
had I not rescued her. You have no honor.
You don't deserve my help. Look, I don't give
a fig if Alex balls the horny bitch
until the cows come home. You deal with it.
I'm out until you make amends. I need
apologies. I need to see you beg."

And so Athena too went cold on Aga's
army. Where was the virgin counselor of
Achilles? At a karaoke bar!
In trousers and a tie, she crooned that night
and broke the hearts of butch and straight alike:

Aga wants my help with crime,
But I'm bidin' my time,
'Cause that's the kind of guy I'm.

As Aga psyched his Raiders to assault
the ramparts of Café Apollo, she
caroused in Mid-Town, sipping gin, relaxing.
It's really true—a tipsy goddess singing
Gershwin in a karaoke bar—
I swear and I should know: I wrote the script
with all the scamp and swagger it deserves.

The gathered men awaited Aga's thoughts.
He swallowed, "My friends, why reinvent the wheel?
We'll make a low-key show of force and let
the Hammer see firsthand that he can't win.
We'll take the conflict home to his own haunt.
Café Apollo's perfect: We can eat
and drink together, relax and wait, and hold
ourselves aloof and bait them with politeness.
A firm but subtle show of strength will rout
their crude behavior."
                              Odysseus then rolled
his eyes as if to say to Nestor, *Daft.*
Has he gone daft? It won't work out that way—
they'll smirk or try to kick our ass, and they
will have the crowd with them. Those crude Martillos
will beat us like piñatas. Odysseus
began to speak, but Aga shut him down
and then ignored the hand sage Nestor raised.
And so the others meekly went along.

As planned, the brigand eight walked in and found
two tables toward the back, but not before

a murmur crossed the room and bar stools scraped
and scuffed as patrons craned to get a look.
First in was giant Ajax, followed close
behind by leader Agamemnon. The buzz
was palpable: Their size and dress set them
apart from regulars in laid-back jeans
and T-shirts. Business casual meant trouble.
Café Apollo was no biker bar,
but it was not the type of place that called
to wealthy slummers or entitled folks.
Then Ajax Kurtz came in and caused a stir
because he looked miscast—as if an unkempt
vagrant had been recruited to the upper
middle class. The patrons to a man
were puzzled. Menelaus changed the take
at once. Though wearing slacks and white dress shirt,
he did not seem benign:
                    A barfly shouted,
"This guy was in a fight here sometime back.
I'm sure. He's the guy who bloodied Alex' face.
He wore a crimson fleece. He's hard to miss.
The red hair too. So what is going down?"
     Odysseus confirmed the speculation:
No matter what their dress, something was
afoot. Like Ajax Gross he was too large
and fit to be a simple patron here
to have a drink. When Nestor, moving slowly,
perhaps it was his age, walked in and then
Idomeneus, dressed in a suit, their presence
did not change the crowd's foreboding sense.
Machaon's entry did not register.
He was respected, but the die was cast.
     Apollo in his office heard the noise
and walked in from the back to find the men
at tables drinking draft Corona Lites.

The dirty war survivor knew at once
the challenge Aga's move implied. Often
Achilles or the Ajax boys would come
alone for drinks. A mutual respect
developed into a truce of equals. They dressed
in jeans and T-shirts, Achilles rode a bike—
so they belonged there in a sense. But when
these ricos came in custom shirts and slacks,
Apollo knew it was a condescending act,
a gauntlet thrown in Hector's face by Aga.
Not wanting more hostilities in his
café, he texted Hector not to come:
"A leak is causing problems and we're about
to close." Yet still Apollo loved a fight—
but mostly as a patron of the winners.
(Only Ares loved a conflict more.)
He racked his brains to find another venue.
Then Hector texted back: "We're there in five
to help with any problems." At once he knew
his only option was to set the rules
to favor Hector. *What bad luck*, he thought.

     Apollo greeted Aga, "Hello, nice
to see you here tonight. What brings you in.
And eight of you! A birthday or event
to celebrate?"

               "Not really," Aga said,
"just out to have a drink and thought a change
of scene would do us good. It's been a while."
     "It has. I hope you're well and prospering."
Of course the god knew every sordid detail.
"Enjoy yourselves. I'm sending empanadas
over on the house. I'll come by later."

     The Hammer was confused when he walked in.
The music was full tilt, the kitchen open.

The place was crowded with the usual—
a mix of locals, artists, hangers-on
out having fun, and women, Montrose types,
some gays. He couldn't find Apollo, so
he reasoned it was a false alarm. And glad
to have the evening now as planned, a night
of camaraderie among themselves,
he called the others in—Alex, and
Agenor and his son, the marked Ekheklos,
Aeneas and Euphorbus, and also suitor
Othryoneus, arrived from out of town.
He had come in to court Cassandra.
                                    Before
a drink was served the night went south. The Hammer—
still brimming rage and pain from Ajax' brick,
a plastic surgeon had wired him together—
first grimaced, grinned, then smirked when he saw Aga
and his assembled minions swapping tales.
His face in knots, he scowled, his nostrils flared,
a lion on the scent of long-sought prey.
Apollo slipped back in, observing things
but keeping in the shadows out of sight.

It might have stopped right there, but Hector spied
vile Ajax Gross at ease in Aga's group.
        He felt his jaw and yelled across the room,
"You scumbag, make my day. Stand up and fight.
I have a score to settle from that night."
        "You chicken shit, you don't deserve the name
'marine.' What ghosts did you bring home? At ease,"
said Gross, and softening, he added, "please, Hector,
I have no quarrel beyond the other night.
Enjoy your friends and let it go."
                                    But Hector
wouldn't have it, "Because of you my mouth

is filled with wire. A fight's a fight but not
with gutter bricks."

Apollo seized control,
and taking him aside, he said, "Not yet,
my friend. Cool it and relax a bit,
and let the ruckus simmer some for now."

The Hammer, not known for his compliance, heeled.
Apollo Fuente ruled his roost. He had
no choice. He hated to be cowed. He was
the Hammer, Hector, Priam's son. Comply?
Not him, but he was bridled by the god's
house rules.

"Look, hold your horses, cowboy, chill.
I'll help you when it's right. *Relajate*."

The Hammer stewed, as Aga's friends caroused,
fressing nachos and guzzling vats of ouzo.
The plot began to ripen in the dark
café beneath the nurture of the strobe lights
and swelled by bodies dancing on the floor.

The next move was Apollo's: Sensing he
could win and randy for a kill, the god
took charge, cranked up the rock, and cut the strobes.

"Now, Hector, move it."

Quick as quarks Martillos
stormed across the room. Still seated, Aga's
men were drinking, guards down for the moment.
The lupine pack, the Hammer's minions, rushed
and swarmed the nested Raiders. No coups could be
assigned: A bottle landed Aga on
the floor, and someone stabbed Odysseus
and left his shirt suffused with his own blood.
Now up, the Raiders fought, but Hector's gang
were vicious, relentless, mean as feral hogs,
so Aga's team was losing ground. Attacks

by them were stymied by Apollo's hand:
Big Ajax tried to hammer Hector's face
a second time when Fuente's god-swift arm
held his aloft, and Hector ducked.

The fight
spilled out into the parking lot where Nestor
(why was retired Nestor present?) caught
a fist thrown by Aeneas. (Had this egregious
act occurred in warring Troy, another
hero would have founded ancient Rome.)
Old Nestor fell and gashed his head against
the concrete. Now Poseidon rose to help
the Raiders with a pelting rain and loosed
loud thunder claps and lightning bolts against
the outside lights and stymied Hector's efforts.
The blackness made it hard to see the havoc.
By luck, a patron spotted Nestor on
the ground, had had enough, and called the police.
Soon sirens wailed all but supplanting thunder,
the shouting, and the music. The noise drowned out
the hope of truce.
Then young Othryoneus,
the greenhorn newbie, spotted Idomeneus,
alone and silhouetted near the dumpster.
He chased him back behind then swung and slashed
his forearm with a broken bottle. Bad move,
young greenhorn. Idomeneus then drew a Glock,
and when he lunged again, he stopped his clock.
The shots were swallowed by confusion. He slid
against the dumpster, crumpled out of view.
At once Idomeneus reholstered it
and joined the other wounded. Approaching squad
cars sent the Raiders homeward—Nestor and

Idomeneus were aided, and all but him
had no idea anyone had died.
For lack of evidence the police would struggle.
Could anyone imagine the well-dressed man
in suit and tie had killed the youthful suitor?

The Hammer did the math. The aftermath:
they savaged four of them—Idomeneus,
Odysseus, old Nestor, Agamemnon.
That's quite a score, the Hammer thought. *Not dead
but bloodied—better than warm bodies.* "At worst,
if caught and charged, it's battery. My friends,
you won the day," the Hammer said. "Perfect,
you pummeled them and sent their asses back
to River Oaks. *Muy bien, muchachos.*"

Why Hector missed that Ajax went unscathed
remains a puzzle, but other matters pressed.
        Dread struck young Alex when he looked around,
"Where's Cassie's suitor, the kid Othryoneus?"
And hearing no response, he shouted to
Apollo Fuente in the parking lot.
        "I haven't seen him either."
                                As they waited,
a gritty mist of fear enveloped them,
abraded their successful rout, and hung
acidic, bristling in the air around
the group.
                Then someone yelled, "A body, God,
a guy's behind the dumpster."
                                Hector knew
at once. "It's murder. Those bastards killed the boy."
        Apollo broke the news, "The kid's been shot."
        The Hammer paced a moment and then spoke:

"This murder changes things. Consider today
round one. My litany of wrongs is long:
the death of Mestor, now the boy, and Ajax,
and don't forget Achilles and Patroclus.
As for the tragedy today, it's hopeless:
the police will be involved, fat chance of justice.
Friends, we must act with all deliberate speed.
Achilles, Agamemnon, Ajax Gross
are fucking killing us. I want revenge.
You want to know why I'm so angry? Listen.
With Mestor we have no proof, but I am sure
it's on Achilles' head, and with the boy
we have an obligation to his parents.
And Gross is second only to Achilles.
Insult, honor, murder draw my fury.

      "But for the moment put aside small things:
my jaw, my pride, the honor of my sister—
you know that Ajax Kurtz is stalking her.
We have to be strategic in our target.
The weakest prey is, strange to say, Achilles.
He lives unguarded with that bird Patroclus—
the one who maimed me—and Briseis. Strong
and cunning but no match for all of us.
He's cocky and his house is unsecured—
if we're to score, the place is surely there.
We must strike hard and take Achilles down,
put fear as well in Aga, and set the cuckold
clucking." One rends a fabric anywhere
and soon it all unravels. "Screw those bastards."

The Biker will be needing counsel soon
to judge from Hector's hate and firm resolve.
Again, where is Athena, virgin goddess?
Still dancing at the karaoke bar

(as chastely as she can). The goddess has
released herself to pleasure. Pleasure. Think
of singing nuns or giddy Hassids dancing.
Or better, since she is a goddess, think
Carmina Burana and the angels singing.

     Another gin and by degrees she falls.
He does not need me now, she thinks, *I'm free*.
Athena loses it and twerks her butt—
a brazen twerk in front of perfect strangers.
I swear it's true, as You-Know-Who's my witness.
The goddess sings a song we cannot hear.
What ecstasy has overtaken her?
What visit to Elysium is planned?

     One half-wit calls to her, "Sing it, baby.
More, more, oh, Athena, *mi amor*,
grab the mic you gorgeous dyke and sing."

BOOK XII. AVICIDE

A few days later at Café Apollo, Hector and the god sit talking. Hector begins to go through his list of grievances, and Apollo cuts him off and reminds him that they've been through his complaints before. When Hector reiterates that he wants revenge, Apollo counsels a more measured approach. They agree that the best first step is to target Achilles, and the two lay out a plan. Apollo cautions Hector to take him captive—not to kill him. Apollo says Hector must develop a truce with Achilles on his own terms and warns against killing Patroclus. Hector and his allies descend on Achilles' house in the dark. He and Euphorbus break in to find only Patroclus at home. Euphorbus encounters him in the kitchen where the macaw attacks him and draws first blood. Hector bursts in, and Patroclus, enraged by Hector's entry and triggered by Briseis' lingerie on the table, attacks him. Eventually Hector subdues the bird, cinches a cord around its neck, and strangles him by whirling him around the room. Hector desecrates the body by severing a foot from Patroclus as a good luck charm and notes that Achilles will understand that by his cutting through the tendon and taking the foot, he is taunting Achilles about his own death. He hangs the corpse from a bridge in full view as if Patroclus were a victim of a Mexican drug cartel's revenge. At home that night he falls into a fitful sleep. Patroclus appears to him and announces that the Fates have decreed his death.

A few days later Apollo Fuente sat
with Hector in a corner over coffee.

"I'm hurting," Hector said, "I know we've been
through this before, but everything's unsettled.
I've got to act decisively right now.
You know the list, indulge me anyway."

"I know your list ad nauseam: Achilles,
then Agamemnon, Ajax. On and on,
it goes. I get it, honestly, I get it.
Remember, I counseled you the other night
when Aga and his guys came taunting you.
I also found the boy, Cassandra's suitor.
I rescued you when Ajax Gross came close
to killing you and blocked his blow right here
in my café. I know you think they're creeps,
and, yes, the police are clueless. You want
to move on this."

"I do. I want revenge.
I want to cut those motherfuckers down."
He ran his hand across his jaw and winced.
"That brick that broke my face," has sealed the fate
of Ajax Gross for sure. I want your help
to end this story on Martillo terms."

"*Tranquilo*, Hector, don't go off half-cocked,"
the God of Light, and flayer of the satyr
Marsyas, suggested. (Fine one to talk.)
"Decide on what you can and cannot do,
what goals are worth achieving and to what end.
Fate will not grant you total satisfaction,
so compromise and focus wisely. Given
that there are no perfect choices, here's one
approach that you can implement:

"As you
remarked, Achilles is the chain's weak link.
The homes of Aga and his brother will

be hard to hit. There's gated fortresses.
The Biker's fierce, I'll grant you that. But still
you got it right the other night. His house
is porous, a craftsman's cottage, a piece of cake—
with no alarm I'd venture. Pride would not
allow him one. It's wood, a single story
in Montrose where shit happens every day,
and no one takes much notice. If there are
enough of you, you'll capture him. Extract
a lasting truce. That's crucial. If you need
a little force, okay. But not so much
that he'll come after you. It's delicate,
a subtle conquest of the spirit. Forget
about vendetta. It's just not going to happen.
I warn you: If you kill Patroclus, as
you plan, try to humble him with pain,
and lord it over him that you're his master,
he'll surely hunt you down and murder you."

    "I thought you were a god, courageous."

    "Nothing but the ego is unbounded,
so get a grip and take what you can get."

    "Okay, you win. You're right, so I accept
your premise. I'm in. The two are both my targets,
Achilles and Patroclus. As for the bird,
I'll wring that no-good motherfucker's neck."

    "My friend, don't say I didn't warn you. I want . . ."

    "Apollo, please, just let me ventilate
a little. I know I have to rein it in.
So I'm on board. I'll follow your advice.
I've also got to make the brothers answer
for the death of Cassie's greenhorn suitor.
And there's Kurtz who's been harassing her.
Yes, I can focus on Achilles as you
suggest, but the actions of the brothers
and their friends need answering as well.

Enough, let's think about Achilles and how
to take him down. I'd like to hear your thoughts."

    Apollo smiled. "I think it's pretty easy.
Your goal is not to kill but apprehend.
The worst result should be a misdemeanor,
although I hope it will not come to that.
Just capture him and we can plan his fate.
I want to go through this again with you.
You murder him and you're as good as dead.
Achilles is from River Oaks. The cops
will hunt you down and see you die in Huntsville.
I've had my say, but once you start, don't fail
or you're dishonored, not to mention dead."
    "Okay, fine, let's talk about a plan."
    "So here's my guide to keep you out of trouble.
Rule one: Take no guns of any kind.
Rule two: Use only loyal, trusted men.
Rule three: Decisive action is essential.
Rule four: A simple plan is best for this.
    "First, borrow a service truck, a panel truck,
one of yours and then paint out the name.
Remove the plates. Remember, check the gas.
Your daily driver's good if you can trust
the man, and have him bring his tools. That way
you'll have the hammers, pliers, crowbars to break
in, sundry stuff, and baling wire to bind
your prey. An electrician's really key. He'll cut
the power. Take Achilles in the dark.
You'll carry heavy-duty flashlights to blind
the man. You'll be surprised how well this works.
Briseis will be at the club. He'll be
alone and maybe plastered. Two of you
should storm the house while others guard the exits

and watch the windows. Tie him, throw him in
the panel truck. and you, my friend, are done.
   "No, wait, I have some army surplus flashlights
for you to take. They're bright as strobes. Remember
to blind him with this searing shaft of light
as if it were the stake Odysseus
once used to quell the Cyclops Polyphemus.
Then bind him like a sacrificial ram.
And do no more to him until we speak.
That clear? I think this simple scheme will work."

Now Hector talked to his assembled men:
Kabriones, the driver, his friend Aeneas,
his brother Alex, whom he had summoned there,
Euphorbus, young and skilled in rumbles, and
illegals—four of them to slither back
to Mexico when done. Apollo sent
Juan Cienfuegos, an electrician friend.
   "I'm asking for your help to heal a wound,"
he said to them. "We must avenge the deaths
of Mestor and the lad Othryoneus."
   A bit extravagant, perhaps, but to
engage the team, he pulled out all the stops:
"*Guerreros* all—my friends and *compañeros*,
and *obreros*, tough illegals at
the ready," was how he rallied them.
                              Then he
explained the caper in detail, "You men,"
he said in Spanish, "will get a thousand dollar
bonus if this works."
                   Not everyone,
not loyal friends Aeneas and Euphorbus—
since they were in for honor, not reward.
   "Tomorrow night we'll meet again at eight.

Here is a layout of Achilles' place.
First Juan will cut the power at the box.
In darkness I'll charge the front with you and you—
he pointed at two Mexicans. We'll smash
the door, then I'll go in, and you will cover
to prevent escape," he said in Spanish
then English. The backdoor is Euphorbus' task.
Aeneas will patrol the rear. The rest
of you will watch the sides. I'll shout for lights
again, and all of you should rush to help.

     And I'll provide the weapons—crowbars, tire
irons, brass knuckles, gloves—a must for all
of you, your DNA would be a calling
card—and also hammers. No guns, *nada*.
Your flashlights are like weapons, use them first.

     "Euphorbus, you're the key. The two of us
can take him and secure him if we work
together, but, and this is crucial, all
of you must hurry in to hold him down.
Your thoughts, your questions? . . . No, okay, remember
a thousand dollar bonus if Achilles
is brought out alive, hogtied, not dead."

Apollo, god of many things, cannot
outmatch Athena or raw Fate, and so
events unfolded in a different way.
(By now Athena was in tiptop shape.)
     It just so happened that Briseis took
the evening off for date night with Achilles,
for even the brave and fair enjoy time out
far from the rigors of heroic life.
We find Briseis in the kitchen with bags
of groceries to put away, a pile

of wash in need of folding, including bras
and panties discretely shunted to the side.
  Before stuff could be shelved and stowed, he says,
"My love, please get your pretty ass in gear.
We're out of here. I'll hit the lights. Patroclus,
my Bird of Paradise, sleep tight but lightly.
I count on you as sentinel in lieu
of dogs, alarms, or booby-traps. Come B.,
we're late. Patroclus, one more thing, the plate
of special brownies on the kitchen table
is off limits. When we get home, like Stein
and Toklas, we'll partake, Briseis too.
N'est-ce pas? For now lay off, you are on duty.
And you my love, my God, you're beautiful,
You ready, B.? Let's go, but under protest.
I'm thinking of the bedroom for romance."
  "What's new? You always do, my love," she smiled.
  Patroclus raged and flared his wings

         "Stop, Bird,
this jealousy has got to stop. I mean it.
We're going out for dinner. Cut us some slack.
When we get home, your time will come. Now chill."
  And out they went and left Patroclus, Bird
of Paradise, forlorn and in the dark.

That night they parked the panel truck out front
and spread out to their stations—all but Alex,
who hung back near the truck and watched. Dainty
Alex. The lights were out, the shades were drawn.
What now? Follow the plan to cut the current,
break down the doors. The Hammer waved to Juan.
His crowbar pried the lock. The hardened steel
was slow to give. At last its innards fell

and clattered. The back was less secure, and so
his man Eurphorbus was the first to enter.
Patroclus cawed. Confused, Eurphorbus torched
the kitchen—nothing, or so it seemed, but soon
Patroclus found the beam and fixed on it
as if a target turned the tables and used
a tracer to find a shooter. He sortied at it
and thrust his claws, attacked, and drew first blood—
he slashed and saber-scarred Euphorbus' nose.

    "Holy shit, you motherfucker, I'll fix . . ."

    Patroclus' beak now pierced the malar flesh
and blood gushed in his eye. He reeled in pain.
Bird landed, pecked his neck. Euphorbus flailed
his arms. A lucky blow—Apollo's torch
smacked Patroclus' head and stunned him. He spiraled
floor-ward, lay undetected in the dark.

    Now through the door frame, Hector charged.

                   "I'm in
the kitchen," called Euphorbus."

               "Where's Achilles?"

    "Damned if I know. Patroclus is back here.
The fucking bird attacked me."

               Around
the living room the Hammer flashed his light,
"Achilles isn't here. I'll search the house."
With stealth he crept from room to room. No one.
"The coward's hiding in a closet. Guard
the doors and windows. He will run."

               Of course
we know he's drinking Chardonnay and laughing.
Briseis has just posed a riddle: "A lion,
a leopard, and a cheetah are in a race.
Which one will win?"

            "I know this one. It's old."

"So what. It's fun. I love this joke. The lion
or the leopard. Cheetah's never win."

In Montrose Hector is about to close
a chapter in our story in a most
unpleasant way. Patroclus is alone
and wounded, and the Hammer gives no quarter
to his enemies. The bird is doomed—
Achilles and Briseis cannot help.
The two besotted lovers will long linger.

"Achilles and Briseis are both out.
That bastard's flown the coop." The Hammer paused.
     Euphorbus shouted, "We have a consolation
prize, Patroclus. Come and get him in
the kitchen."
                Now the bird was flying but
more slowly. Clearly hurt and dazed, he swooped
and feinted like an injured wide receiver.
     The Hammer called the men outside to help
him take the bird and yelled to Juan, "Turn on
the lights, right now."
                     The men streamed in. Patroclus
cawed and circled.
                "My mistake. Please leave
the kitchen, all of you! This chaos aids
Patroclus' mockery of our intent.
The two of us can handle this alone.
And close the door. I'm going to kill the bastard."
     With that he grabbed a broom and swatted at
the bird and missed the capeless matador.
He swung. This time he knocked some dishes off
the sink and sent shards flying helter skelter.
Patroclus saw Briseis lingerie
and found the strength to rush at raging Hector—

a replay of the office scene. The bird
of old seemed back. He tried to slash the Hammer
but crashed instead into the fridge. Then Hector
swung and hit the bird athwart, a blow
so smart it knocked Bird to the floor. He lunged,
went sprawling on the glass, and grabbed
the bird who bit him on the hand. He cursed,
but now he had a better purchase.

      "Euphorbus,
quick, the rope." With one fist Hector snatched
the claws and bundled them. The other held
the body to the floor. That left the beak
to peck at him. Somehow he found a way
to make a slipknot of the cord, a noose,
and as he struggled to ensnare the neck,
the bird attacked his hand.

      "You motherfuck,
you die."

   He fixed the noose and motioned back
Euphorbus, cinched it, and softball deft, he pitched
the bird aloft and slowly spun him. Slowly,
slowly. Just enough to choke a bit
and guide its course. At first it seemed the bird
was flying round and round, as if a child
were playing in the park, but as the speed
increased, the flapping ceased. The Hammer's face
was all sardonic grimace. Faster, he whirred
the bird apace. Euphorbus felt the wind.
They heard a snap and knew the task was done.
But faster, faster still, he spun the bird,
himself half-crazed, imagining Achilles
orbiting around him. Now Hector saw
the bras and panties on the table and felt
the shame of both attacks. A hateful rictus

beset his face which hid his gnawing wound.
He whipped Patroclus harder round the room.

"Stop it, Hector, stop, you're mad. It's just
a dead macaw, that's all," Euphorbus said.
        "I'll quit, but it's not over. Achilles loved
Patroclus, cherished him—much more than men
adore their dogs. Patroclus made him glow.
Note, I say 'made' not 'makes.' It's our advantage."
The bird lay wrung out at his feet. "Achilles
will want to bury him. Watch this. He'll not
get all of him, no way. I'll have my charm
from flesh, a lucky talisman, much better
than a rabbit's foot." He took a clever,
let out a yelp, and, thwack, he whacked through bone
and tendon at the "ankle," which left a claw
and tarsal trophy. Then he spit on him.
        "Achilles will not fail to notice how
the tendon is transected at the heel.
I'll take this to a taxidermist, have him
surmount the tip with silver, and wear the foot
looped through my belt and taunt Achilles. Each time
he sees me, he'll go mad with hate. Revenge,
how sweet, when wronged by naked rage or Fate."

They were about to leave when Hector paused.
A look came over him. "I'll cripple him.
I'll fix his wagon," and he slashed the tires
of his bike. They hustled from the scene.
Kabriones drove to an urgi center.
They dropped Euphorbus off with Alex for
a tetanus shot and stitches then headed north
on Waugh unsure of what to do. They drove
and grumbled. Then crossing over Allen Parkway,

he thought about the bridge in Monterrey
with corpses strung up by a drug cartel—
a warning not to fuck with them. *Why not,*
he thought, *rebuke Achilles with that specter?*
Next railroad tracks—ka-plunk. On Heights before
I-10 there was a half-forgotten bridge—
a pristine relic—over White Oak Bayou.

"Stop here, right here. We'll string him up right here."
He slung Patroclus' body over and
secured the cord so that he swung above
the water by his neck, abandoned and
forlorn. He told the four *obreros* to
stand watch and keep away the rats and bums,
the curious—two men by turn in shifts.
He or Aeneas would come by to check.
        Café Apollo welcomed them for beers.
There Hector figured how to let the Biker
know the site of his humiliation.

That night at home the Hammer tossed and turned
in fitful sleep. A great white-sheeted fog
enveloped him, a silent void where mist
and vapors spiraled upward. Furtively
they swirled, then gathered speed and funneled to
a viscous fluid cone congealing as
a bird—Patroclus, white against the black.
The gyrating mass solidified, was still,
a lone macaw that sucked the whiteness to
itself.
        Then flaring wings in rage, Patroclus
presaged the Hammer's death, "I tend my soul
tonight. Achilles will find and honor me.
You'll fail. You cannot desecrate my body.

The Fates will not permit it. He will find
you too, and when he does, he'll murder you.
You'll die in shame and disregard, disgraced,
dishonored, a coward, alone, unnurtured and
disheveled. Apollo cannot reverse the Fates'
demands, Athena's wishes. You unholy
swine, get ready, you're as good as dead."

Then Hector, the Hammer, woke with fright and knew.

BOOK XIII. SKIRMISH AT WHITE OAK BAYOU

ARGUMENT. Achilles and Briseis return from dinner to find the front door open and the house in disarray. Patroclus has vanished, and Achilles immediately suspects Hector. He calls Agamemnon to make amends and ask for help finding Patroclus. The conversation is interrupted by a text message directing Achilles to a YouTube video, which shows Patroclus' body hanging from a bridge over White Oak Bayou, and taunting Achilles to come and take it. Agamemnon and Achilles don't much like each other, but honor, class, and common cause bring them together and elicit apologies, though Achilles harbors reservations. Along with Agamemnon, Menelaus, Ajax Gross, Ajax Kurtz, and Meriones, he sets out for the bridge. When they arrive, Achilles and Agamemnon stay back with the cars. The others encounter Hector, Aeneas, and the four hired Mexicans. A fight ensues. Gross dispatches the Mexicans, and he and Kurtz hold Hector and Aeneas at bay while Menelaus and Meriones recover Patroclus' body and return with it to the cars. Achilles is disconsolate at his companion's death. Gross alerts Briseis who prepares the house for their arrival. They sit solemnly and share a drink. Achilles swears he'll avenge Patroclus' death by killing Hector. After the men leave, he notices that Hector has taken one of Patroclus' claws. Further enraged, he swears to keep his word to kill the Hammer. He falls into a trance-like state and hears a voice from his motorcycle say that he himself will not live long: The killing of Mestor and his wife have denied him a hero's life and a hero's death.

The doors ajar, a window fully wedged
was how Achilles and Briseis found
the house on their return.
                    "Patroclus, dear
Patroclus, are you okay? We're home, my Bird. . . .
Patroclus, where are you? Please. In the kitchen?"
       Dead silence rifled back.
                      Briseis cried,
"Don't torment us, Patroclus. Fly out, come here."
       The disarray was clear—nothing stolen,
but chairs were overturned, and drawers were open.
No caw or crow, nor winning flap of wings.
The air was still. Nothing moved. Deep dread
abraded him as if a steel wool brush
had scrubbed the chambers of his heart.
                          "He's gone,

Briseis. Hector's holding him, I'm sure.
That no-good bastard's history, dog food.
The stupid SOB's abducted him.
He'll stop at nothing to get back at me.
We've got to free Patroclus."
                  He called Aga:
"I need your help. I'd like to put aside
our feud. We have a common enemy
in Hector's clan. Patroclus was abducted—
he's gone without a trace. It makes no sense.
Hold on, wait just a sec. I've got a text. . . .
What's this? A YouTube link, a video.
It's from an unknown number. Later, friend."

In disbelief the Biker and Briseis
looked in horror: Patroclus dangled limp
below a bridge, a noose around his neck,

a ghost submerged in blackness. Then Hector's voice,
"Patroclus fucked with me the day you came
to threaten me. Go fuck yourself, Achilles."
    Then next appeared a "Come and Take It" flag—
the one the Texans at Gonzáles flew
defiantly—draped across the bridge.
And that was it, a thirty-second clip.
    "He's dead, Briseis, dead, our friend is dead.
Hector will die a brutal death, I promise,
but first things first. I must retrieve Patroclus—
I need to offer prayers and bury him.
A waste, a wanton, vengeful, senseless waste."

He called back Aga in despair, "That fuck
has killed Patroclus, hung his body from
a bridge. I think it's over White Oak Bayou.
I'm in, I'm really in. We'll have the head
of Hector shortly. Once settled, we'll lay waste
to everything Martillo. I have to bring
Patroclus back. I'm sure that Hector has
not left the site unguarded. I'll need some help.
I know that Gross and Kurtz are in. I'll call,
but can I count on you and Menelaus?"
    "Truth is, Achilles, you're not an easy guy
to like, but you're courageous—I'll give you that.
We have a common enemy, and, well,
you're one of us. Your mother lives nearby.
I know your father. So for better or
for worse, our lives are bound to one another's.
We need to talk about Briseis too,
but for the moment let's set that aside.
And we have other issues—Helen and
our stock, your voting seat, but they can wait
as can the arrogance of Hector's clan.

Of course we'll help, Achilles. We'll do what's
needed. May I suggest Meriones,
our friend? He's plenty tough and trustworthy."
        "Sounds good, the six of us can get this done."
        "We'll swing by and pick you up at eight."

When Agamemnon came that night, he found
Achilles pacing in the drive.
                                He blurted,
"I'm desperate. I need to find Patroclus.
It's gnawing at my innards like a cancer.
That bastard's crude, vindictive. Look at this—
as if Patroclus' death were not enough,
the Hammer slashed a brand-new set of tires."
        "Be cool, relax, my friend. We'll set this right."
        Achilles pulled a tire iron from
a saddle bag and brandished it—the very
one he used on Mestor and his wife.
He glared as he got into Aga's car.
His brother Menelaus followed with
Meriones and Ajax Gross and Kurtz.
        "Just head out Waugh to White Oak, Aga, and
we'll have a look."
                        "I'm glad to help and pleased
we are alone to talk a bit. Somehow
the time was never right. Let's call it what
it is. We've had our differences, but I
own some of this. So hear me out. I have
wronged you. Apologies, Achilles, I'm
remiss. Sincere, heart-felt apologies.
I rue the day I took Briseis. I had
no right to her. Desire stole my mind.
Insanity absconded with my wits.
Stupidity eroded my good sense.
And now I must admit I am ashamed

for both our clans. I sundered trust and honor.
In part that's why I make amends with help
to find Patroclus. What I did was wrong—
I guess I feel I must atone with deeds
that count. Another thing, your love, Briseis,
I never laid a hand on her. Ask her,
I swear it's true. Let's put this all behind us.
Our first task is to find Patroclus' body."

It's hard to read Achilles' take on this—
though as he thought, Athena hovered near.
The speech was long, and Aga almost groveled.
What's that supposed to mean? I'm missing something.
We can imagine the jungle fighter was
pragmatic, that he shrewdly played along
because he sorely needed Aga's help:
"I thank you for your thoughts. How can a man
like me not understand that evil can
suffuse our consciousness, take over and
commandeer our souls? Napoleon
smothers Gandhi in my dreams each night.
Stark honesty demands I see both good
and evil mingled in my heart and deeds."
       Perhaps Athena, overhearing, thought,
I'm stunned, there may be hope for that boy yet,
but nothing's harder than to know a god's
intent. Let's listen to Athena's thoughts.
Here is Achilles channeling to Aga:
"None of this is easy, Aga. Thank you.
To own our faults is to admit a wound.
You're generous in coming forward so.
I take your points. Apology accepted."

Yet did he find self-knowledge when
Athena held his thoughts? We cannot know.

Perhaps Achilles faced an ugly truth:
Again and again he would betray his fellow
human beings—Aga and every other
person on this planet—and given time
and motive, they would do the same. Was this
a truth that he accepted, one he deeply
owned? For now, this Aga seemed sincere,
contrite—and maimed Achilles had no choice.

They saw I-10 and cut their lights then parked
close by the bridge.
                    "Achilles, you wait here
with me. We'll put Patroclus in their care."
        With Menelaus the others headed for
the bridge. Big Ajax Gross went first, ice pick
in hand and backed by Ajax Kurtz who waved
a sawed-off shotgun. They sprang and rushed the ruck,
the others right behind. The six defenders—
the Mexicans and Hector and Aeneas—
were caught off guard. Gross grabbed the flag and hooded
one, then kicked him in the groin, and tossed
him.
        "Come and take it," little Ajax cried
and fired a warning blast.
                        Big Ajax jammed
his pick into another's arm and floored
him with a cross. The other *vatos* ran.
Cowed Hector and Aeneas shrank—this Gross
was rapier fast and diamond hard. Kurtz fired
a second warning shot. Meriones
watched Menelaus hoist the body up,
then cut the stanchioned cord and cradle him,
and without pause he whisked Patroclus back.
That ugly rope, which trailed, the hangman's noose,
now scudded in their wake along the pavement.

Resolve returned to Hector, who charged the two.
    "Come closer, and I'll turn your face to *salsa
roja*. If you doubt me, come." He stopped,
not sure of Kurtz's courage, "Despicable,
you useless turd, you chicken shit."
                            Next Gross
let fly a martial throwing star, but Hector
adroitly dodged the whirr and cursed them both.
They turned, and racing for the cars, all four
arrived at once. Then Menelaus laid
Patroclus on a crimson carpet that
Aga had unfurled in the back
of his sedan. Achilles wobbled, grabbed
the car door, hung on ashen in despair.
He swallowed and let out a piercing sigh.
Without a word he picked Patroclus up,
rocked his beloved in his arms and kissed
the broken neck. He got back in, and that's
the way he bore the soldier's body home—
his friend and fallen comrade in his arms.
He stroked the dirty plumage, sobbed at loss,
and cursed the Hammer and the needless carnage.

The "needless carnage" phrase was pure Athena,
who worked to cool Achilles' molten rage
and sluice a softness to the Biker's heart.
She was a countervailing force for calm
though not enough to slake his lust for blood.
The magma lodged below preferred revenge,
and no amount of reason could reverse
the thrust of the Avenger's hateful fury.

Discreetly from the second car, Big Ajax
called Briseis.

"Oh, no," she screamed. "My poor
Achilles, poor Patroclus. Oh, no, no, no.
Please call my love to let him know I know
and tell him all of you are welcome back.
We need to gather even though the hour
is late."
　　　　　She struggled to be strong for him.
She raced to tidy up, made coffee, tea,
set out a small repast and drink. She chose
the funeral lament from Mahler's "Titan."
Now get a grip, she thought—Dry eyes. And rouge
and lipstick. Later we can grieve in private.
What else? A candle surely, no two, no three.
Startled, she heard the gravel driveway churn,
and lit the candles, hit the CD switch,
and rushed to greet her lover at the car.
Achilles sat in shock.
　　　　　　　　　　"Come in, my love,
the rest of you as well. Please stay a bit
and be with us as we take stock and mourn."
She hoisted him and touched her fingers to
his face and hugged him. "I'm truly sorry, love."
　　　　Then tenderly she took the bird and in
the kitchen placed him on the countertop.
With special care she cleaned the grime and gravel
and sponged his head. Then she saw the severed leg,
and gasped. *He must not see this sacrilege.*
She covered the torso with a kitchen towel,
and in the dining room she laid him out
in state. The men passed by respectfully
in silence. A few fixed plates, but most just poured
a scotch or bourbon and found their seats. In tears
Achilles eyed Patroclus, sobbed, and turned
toward Hector's evil noose, the hangman's snare,

that Ajax had removed and brought inside.
     He held the cord aloft and broke his silence,
"This instrument of death that took Patroclus'
breath, I promise, will be the means of my
revenge. Soon craven Hector will feel the tug
of death himself. I'll cinch this fetid rope
around his neck and slowly tighten it
until I crack his windpipe. His eyes will bug,
his face will flush, his veins will bulge
and leave his neck a swarm of writhing snakes.
The man will suffer as Patroclus did.
I swear to you tonight that Hector's death
will lack the honor that he dearly craves."

     "This night, dear friends, is sad as any I
recall," began Briseis. "We—Achilles
and I—have lost a friend, a love. I know
it's hard to think a bird a person, but
Patroclus was unique. He felt like family.
Patroclus shared our moments good and bad.
That's why three candles are set out tonight.
The three of us have been entwined—as if
we were a holy trinity." She looked
around apologetically and paused,
"I promise I mean no blasphemy by this.
Some days I felt communion with a world
beyond our ken simply by his presence. . . .
Enough of sadness for one evening.
Achilles and I will host a proper service
within the week. As you can see, he needs
a day or two." She looked at him and tears
welled up. "I guess that I do too. Some humor—
let's end the evening on a lighter note:
So in the Scottish Play what should one say
to the fated words that doomed Macbeth?

Recall the scene: 'Fear not, till Birnam wood
do come to Dunsinane.' Ideas? . . . No . . .
'Dear soldiers, to you a hardy "copse vobiscum."'
Good night, Sweet Princes, thank you one and all."

The men had gone. He bore Patroclus' corpse
to the garage and set him down. He looked
in disbelief. "My God, his claw is gone,"
he shouted to Briseis who came running.
"The bastard's mutilated him. He's cut
away his foot and desecrated him.
You've heard my oath already. I stand by it:
I swear the Hammer is as good as dead."
        "My love, you know I am a woman who
would like to counsel prudence and restraint,
but now it's time to act. Be careful though,
and plan revenge to leave no evidence."
        She kissed him, held him, and left him to his task.
        He wrapped the body she had washed and placed
it in the freezer by the workbench. Then
he stood not knowing what to do. He had
no rites for comfort. Disbelief now surged
across his mind without resolve. His friend
must have a fitting burial. Disgrace,
he must festoon the Hammer with disgrace,
no matter what the cost. He had no choice.

A chilling terror rose in him and stripped
away coherence. From the void there came
a resonance between his bike and soul
as if they shared Hell's taproot vector down.
        He heard a voice drift out and draw him in,
"Achilles, you will surely die. Your death
has long been certain. After Hector, you.

You will not live to see a marriage to
Briseis or those children. You had hoped
to live a hero's life and die in glory:
The deaths of Mestor and his wife are cause
for you to forfeit both. Patroclus' death
and mutilation foreshadow your destruction."
    Achilles' body shuddered trying to
shake off the dream's intent, annul the message.
His brain was addled as the specter of
his death now rattled round his head and set
his mind to searching elsewhere for the cause.
In ratchet steps he headed for the house
and cowered as if a truncheon-wielding sadist
had beaten him about the face and head,
then, shaken, slid in bed beside Briseis.

BOOK XIV. THE BIKER KILLS THE HAMMER

ARGUMENT. With Patroclus' body in the garage freezer awaiting burial, Achilles takes the cord that Hector used to strangle him and begins the hunt for the Hammer. Outside BrioBrio he sits on his idling motorcycle and again hears the voice that seems to emanate from it reminding him that though he may kill Hector, he too will shortly die. Achilles imagines he can avoid dishonor by avenging Patroclus' death. At Café Apollo he runs into Agenor and his friends. As he threatens them, Poseidon sends a storm and floods the street sending everyone outside. Across the street at Boutique Cythera, Athena disguised as Henrietta Markham, a sultry young writer, shows up to ask Aphrodite's help with lingerie. The two get into a catfight and Athena/Henrietta bangs Aphrodite's head against the wall and shames her by pricking her butt with an ice pick. Achilles roughs up Agenor as a warm up for Hector. Athena tries to talk him out of the vendetta killing; after all, Patroclus is "only a bird." When Achilles finds Hector, the Hammer runs. At first Apollo thwarts Achilles. But eventually with Athena's help he corners him. Hector tries to bargain for his honor, but Achilles will have none of it and garrotes him. He takes the body back to his house where he finds Patroclus' foot hung from Hector's belt and in fury desecrates his body by grinding his foot into his face. He and Briseis know he will die, and she bitterly reproaches him for not providing for his mother and her.

Achilles, the Avenger, and friend from boyhood
of Patroclus, Bird of Paradise—
still in the freezer awaiting sacred rites
that will release him from his earthly death
to paradise—now roamed the town in search
of Hector. Achilles only took the noose
that Hector used to choke Patroclus and left
his gun, brass knuckles, tire iron home.
At BrioBrio he asked for Hector, but
the girls were giddy since the tips that day
were good and chortled that they had not seen
the Hammer or any of his friends. But would
Achilles like a sample of their wares?
     "No thanks, I'm on the wagon with Briseis.
If you see Hector, call me on my cell.
For him, it's nothing less than life or death."

Then there it was again. He sat astride
his bike near BrioBrio, the engine idling,
and like the other night he heard a voice.
A voice, Achilles, really? Have you gone daft?
It rose from somewhere near the cylinders,
as if a ghost embedded there by Fate
had wanted to expand the prior message.
     "Achilles," it seemed to say, "you may kill Hector,
yet not escape unscathed. Your death will come
much sooner than you think."
                  Oh, get a grip.
You need not tell a soul, not even B.
your bike is warning you, he thought.
Weird shit, this really can't be happening.
I'll get my friend Athena to weigh in.
     His face contorted, he bit his lip. What now?
What choice? *I must avenge Patroclus' death—*

that's first. It's better to die than be dishonored.
He laughed: *My death or my dishonor, really?*
This is a lousy part I have to play—
the poet better give me better lines.
If not, I'll quit and leave his shit unspoken.

The Biker's luck was good—or bad perhaps,
depending on your point of view. At Café
Apollo drinking scotch, Agenor sat with cronies.
    Achilles, spoiling for a fight, stopped by.
"You weren't at BrioBrio. I had hoped
to maim you there or worse. I had bad luck,
but Fate now smiles on me, Agenor. All
of you, my shit-faced friends, are done in by
the Scottish curse of too much single malt.
Before I send you fellows bloodied to
the ER, tell me where that coward is."
    Agenor had no chance to answer him—
a ruckus rolled in from the street.
                    "My god,
there's water everywhere," some boozer shouted.
    Besotted patrons stumbled out to see.
It was the doing of Poseidon. From
the fountain in the yard of Thetis, he willed
a water main to break and flood the street.

But let's roll back the story twenty minutes.
The murder of Patroclus and the brawl
at White Oak Bayou polarized the gods,
who soon took sides and rallied in deed behind
the Hammer or the Biker.
                  Gray-eyed Athena,
the most cerebral of the gods, and with
Poseidon most committed, jumped to back

Achilles and to punish Dite, who'd
helped Helen flee to Paris and begin
the whole shebang (if we forget about
sly Eris who begot the rancor three
millennia ago). Athena took
the guise and garb of Henrietta Markham,
a sultry Boston girl in need of help—
the heft the bras that Dite made might well
provide. Café Apollo was a spit
away.

      "I saw your sign," Athena said,
"'Boutique Cythera' and figured you could help
a girl who moved here recently. I am
a writer and need support for an affair.
Perhaps, some frilly bras and thongs or matching
panties."

        "I don't think we're for you. We are
a high-end shop and cater to a crowd
that's wealthy. Clients don't arrive in jeans
and fraying sweatshirts."

          "What's your problem, sweetie?
My friend likes sexy lingerie on me.
He'll pay the tab. The money's not the issue."

      "All right, my name is Aphrodite. All
of this is mine. Come to the back and let
me see." Once there, she said, "Take off your top.
The changing room is there." When done, she said,
"My God, you need my help. I understand . . .
well, you're . . ."

        "No call for being rude. I know
I'm mini-stacked. Let's go from there."

          "I'm, ah,
sorry. It just slipped out, but in my shop
they're no holds barred. . . . I call them as I see them—

a diagnosis then a planned solution."

"You're blunt, but let's be honest, more is better,"
Athena said. "I bet the rich, the folks
from River Oaks, get better treatment."

"You want my help or not? If not, just leave.
If you decide to stay, it is my way.
That clear?"

"I don't know who you are or why
you're such a hostile bitch," Athena said,
"but you're about to get a lesson in
humility."

She pulled an ice pick from
her bag and lunged. Quick Aphrodite parried,
dispatched it to the floor, and smacked Athena.
They struggled like two schoolgirls in detention
and pulled each other's hair and clawed, though soon
the gray-eyed goddess got the upper hand
and banged the other's head against the wall.
Her blood, Olympic blood, was spattered on
them both. They landed in a tangled knot.
The owner struggled free and staggered to
her feet. She was a sight—her hair still blond
but streaked with bloody red. He blouse was open—
the girl had ripped three buttons off. She ran,
and at the door she shouted, "Help, come quick,
an ice pick-wielding crazy is about
to kill me. Help, please help."

Apollo Fuente,
outside to take the air and smoke his pipe,
caught sight of bloody Dite at the door
and ran across the street. Then somehow they
corralled the girl, who held them off, ice pick
in hand (clad only in a bra and jeans).
Just then, in ways known only to the Fates,

Poseidon eased Athena's plight and loosed
the flood that brought the café's patrons out
into the street and traffic to a halt.
Confusion reigned. Athena pricked the butt
of Aphrodite, let out a whoop, and pick
in hand, triumphant, no exultant, ran.

Agenor and his friends got up, and out
they went. Then drunk as coots, they laughed and drooled,
and one guy bent and grabbed a Wendy's wrapper
floating by. Agenor though stood back—
his Allen Edmond shoes stayed spiffy clean.
Achilles spoiling for a fight went out
and spotted him cavorting near the curb.
Not ready yet for Hector, he rezipped
his jacket to secure the rope and menaced
half-drunk Agenor, seizing his lapels
and spinning him around.
                                        "A lucky night
for you, my friend, relax, I'll kill you when
I'm ready. But a foretaste now." He pressed
both thumbs against the weasel's hyoid bone
above the larynx. Agenor's eyes bugged out.
"Congrats, first-class exophthalmos!" He gagged.
"Well done, Agenor, kudos. Now a bath,
but first this perk." He slapped him hard across
the cheek, and then for fun he tweaked his nose.
"Enjoy the healing waters." He picked him up
and tossed him to the currents. "Farewell, Agenor
of pinstripe suits and fancy-schmancy shoes."
        The other dandies started for the crowd.
No way Achilles would miss his sport with them.
He grabbed two by their locks, expensive mops,
and knocked their heads together. "Coconut

meet coconut. Here's once and twice and thrice
since three's the charm." He flung the groggy fops
into the gutter waters.

           "We are winning,
Achilles." It was Athena bragging on
their acts. "You grabbed those fops, and sent
their mops into the bilging street. As for
that well-born thorn, that busty beauty of
Cythera, I pricked her bubble with a pick."
Such was her burble in Achilles' brain.
"I knew she'd be abusive when I came
in jeans to shop, faux-clueless and flat-chested.
And sure enough, she was. I drew first blood.
I conked her noggin smartly, ready for
an ER doc to stitch. Then Fuente came
and rescued her, but not before I pricked
her little bottom. In fact I gigged her good.
I'm not supposed to say such things. 'I gigged
her good' is not the way a goddess speaks,
but what the hell, no one is privy to us."

"Athena, stop. I need to take my task—
my obligation to Patroclus—on.
For me the Hammer's death and his dishonor
loom paramount."

           "You'll have my help, of course,
but suck it up and don't expect my voice
to whisper in your ear. And as a soldier,
remember, you have a rendezvous with death,
Achilles, one way or the other."

                "I must
uphold the honor of my friend Patroclus."

    "You might try getting real: Patroclus is
a bird, a parrot, no matter what you think.

You are at sea, an engineer awash
in misconstruction. The calculus applied
by you is differential, your reasoning
deductive. You need an integral approach.
The Hammer is already shorn of honor. Yours
are muddled thoughts of tribal retribution.
The noose that Hector used to kill Patroclus—
that which you plan to use on him—is yours
as well. So follow your bliss, but to the abyss."
    She lowered her voice to just a wisp of air,
"A thousand pardons, Joseph Campbell, one
for every hero's face. I repossessed
a line you gave us freely. Sorry I
abused your thought and wrenched its substance free."
    And to Achilles, "There's no chance for glory,
not here, nor anywhere. A whirlwind's caught
you in its blitz—the grit kicked up now clouds
your judgment. Give it up, go home. Briseis
awaits. Take pleasure in the ordinary."

He had no chance to think her offer over—
not that Achilles often listened to
his inner voice—for striding down the street
in combat boots and khaki, Hector came.
He saw Achilles, and about to bolt,
he paused and blinked as if a semaphore
was signaling distress. At this Apollo
cut the line of sight between the two,
and zephyr-footed Hector turned and ran.
    "You're on, Achilles, go," Athena said.
"In Argentina there were beasts like you,
unquenchable for blood, unbridled lust
for human misery, revenge for slight

affronts. Now go chase Hector down, but know
your dirty war will end your days in shame."

He lit out after him past tattoo shops,
boutiques and stores, four other coffee shops
around the block—a hippodrome of wheeze
and puff, though both were fit and strong. Three times
around the block they went. The patrons and
the gods and goddesses were stunned at Hector's
stamina and speed. Achilles raced
in vain. Then gray-eyed Fate, his friend, stepped up:
The Hammer tripped and sprawled. He landed at
a tarot reader's on a quiet street.
Achilles sprung full force, and leopard quick
he dragged him to his feet.
                              "Now, Hector, stand.
Your death's at hand. You know as well as I
your fate. You killed the one I valued more
than any but Briseis, and for that
you will pay dearly."
                        "Want to bet, Achilles?
I've got a Glock. Take stock and deal with that.
My finger's itching to recycle you.
I'll kill you fair and square. I have not doubt,
but I propose a pact whereby we each
agree to heroes' honors for the other
and the return of bodies to our kin.
For after all we both are warriors—
soldiers —and value custom, duty, honor."
      "I can't believe I'm hearing this abuse.
What's this? It's crap you speak, pure garbage, dreck,
the kind of shit you hear from fearful scum.
You are no more a soldier than was Judas.

Once I kill you—I promise that I will—
I'm going to hack you up and pack you up
in tidy plastic garbage bags with ties,
for you are garbage, *mierda*, pure and simple.
I'll drive your pieces north toward Navasota
and scatter you for feral hogs to eat.
You will be barbecue for swine post haste."

Cold fear filled Hector's eyes and paralyzed
his hands. The Glock stayed holster-stashed, pure schlock
against the Biker's rage at lost Patroclus.
It froze the Hammer to a mannequin:
stalagmite-still he stood. Out came the cord
the Hammer used.

        "Please don't, Achilles, I'll
do anything you ask."

        "Then bring Patroclus
back. Now. . . . What? No?"

        He flung the rope around
his neck—garroted him right there. It was
an execution—crude, effective, without
finesse. He cinched the rope as tight as he
was able. Agenor's bug-eyed features crossed
the Hammer's face. He twitched, went slack, and twitched
again. His ruddy face turned cordovan.
His tongue hung out and dribbled frothy slobber.
He crossed his eyes and peed his desert khakis.
A last reflexive jerk helped raise both hands,
which tried to loose Patroclus' cord. Life spent,
he slipped to vermicelli limp and died.

He stopped, not sure of what to do or where
to go? . . . *Get Hector out of here at once.*
He scooped the body up and yoked it on

his shoulders, grabbed an arm and leg. What luck,
no one in sight! He trotted off to find
his bike, then dumped the body in the sidecar.
More luck—the street was black as pitch—the coast
was clear. He'd take the body home and drop
the Hammer in the horizontal freezer.
        In the garage he saw the ghastly claw
that Hector hung as talisman and taunt.
        "You fucking bastard. Now you'll see my brand
of desecration." With that he ground his heel
in Hector's face and stripped Patroclus' claw
from Hector's belt. "I've just begun with you."

Triumphant, into the house he strode and found
Briseis. "Done. I caught him on a Montrose
side street and used the noose he used. Grim work,
good work."
        "Where is he now?"
                                "The outside freezer.
I've lodged him there—the vanquished with the victim,
malicious Hector and our poor Patroclus."
        "Achilles, love, I don't know what we'll do.
You're spent and soaring both at once, and proud.
Yes, you avenged Patroclus, but what's next?
What course to take? We'll bury him, but then?
Forensic evidence will point the trail
to you. No way will you go undiscovered.
They'll hunt you everywhere until they find
your lair—the city police and county police,
Martillos and cartels in league with them.
They'll swarm the land, these vermin—all of them.
You know I'm right in this. Whatever will
we do? What will become of me and Thetis?"
        "As you say, the thing we need to do

is put to rest Patroclus. I know the risks.
I have prepared myself."
                              "But me? Your mother?
And what have you prepared for those you love?"
         "Nothing. Why me? You two and Priam, all,
must act Fate's parts. There's no assuring pact."
         There's no assuring pact, she thought, and then
at once she saw—as if some god had raised
her up to light—his ramrod sense of honor
that precluded love, real love, that drove
the man berserk. She realized his rage
was limbic but in context, that love could not
bore to his Self and see its power wrought.
His molten center swirled about a core
of plasma that was bio-id, not more,
and failing ways to act real manhood's call,
he was alone and overwhelmed by all.
         "So you've betrayed us by omission and
ignored the two most precious in your life.
What honor is there in a man like you?
You love a parrot more than you love us.
What hero's life is this that so lacks grace?
I pledge to help you with Patroclus' rites,
for I admit we share a love of him,
but really there are limits. He's a bird,
a fucking bird, and you're a goddamn fool.
So stop and think. What makes a man disown
humanity? Yes, I'll help bury him,
but after that I'm done. You're on your own,
Achilles. I have a sure and certain hope
Fate fucks you over in a special way."

BOOK XV. SIX AND A HALF WAYS OF HONORING A WHITE MACAW

ARGUMENT. Still consumed by hatred for Hector, Achilles is unable to focus on Patroclus' funeral. Nestor and Odysseus stop by and console him. His spirits lifted and aided by the inner direction of Athena, he imagines a tribute in avian voices, and as he channels Athena, he decides to riff on a Wallace Stevens theme: Thirteen Ways of Honoring a White Macaw. Nestor, Odysseus, and Achilles come up with the requisite thirteen parts, which they and Briseis will present. Nestor begins to have reservations— the service is inappropriate—and tries to get Achilles to recognize that Patroclus is only a bird. He suggests a less grandiose remembrance. Athena, who is eavesdropping, agrees. Achilles is incensed and rejects Nestor's caution. Achilles prepares Patroclus' body. As the guests arrive to Ralph Vaughn Williams' "The Lark Ascending," Achilles greets them. Then Nestor talks about a novel, *Cosmos*, in which a sparrow is garroted and hung up publicly— like Patroclus—thus excoriating Hector and amplifying the meaning of the rites. After other presentations, and halfway through, again disguised as Henrietta Markham, Athena interrupts his speech: Achilles has parrot fever and needs Olympic tetracycline; these rites cannot go on. Aphrodite intrudes, and Athena puts her in her place. Athena tells Achilles not to try to act independently: He needs to pull the plug on Hector in the freezer, give up Briseis, and submit to anima replacement therapy.

Achilles, brilliant engineer, was stuck.
He sat so agitated and forlorn,
despairing, he could not concentrate, could not
construct a service honoring Patroclus.
He wanted something dignified and simple
to convey the loyalty and warmth,
the wit, the raptor courage, and the love
Patroclus lavished on him and Briseis.
Head down he sat as progress darted from him.
Beneath decorum's scab and honor's crust
the magma of his snake-brain core still churned
much fiercer than his civil discipline.
        His limbic system smoldered, and soon
small glimmers of defiance ruptured thought:
revenge, the necessary desecration
of the Hammer's body would redress
the good Patroclus. He could see the corpse
of Hector chopped to pieces, neatly wrapped
in butcher paper, then dumped at Priam's door.
Well, no, in butcher paper stashed in lockers
from Columbus to Port Arthur—in short,
a plan revised in rage, revised again.
        And so when Nestor and Odysseus
came by to buoy his mood, their tenderness
helped cleanse the maggot-fester of his wound,
and they began to plan a fitting tribute.

"Dear friends, I need your help with services
to honor in a proper way a friend
and fallen comrade, one that grasps his warmth
and grace, preserves his granite character
and ancient heritage. I'm at a loss . . ."
        Athena heard, took pity, suffused her charge,

and lit a counter fire, quenching rage
and bringing focus to Patroclus' rites.

From his unconscious bubbled up a vision.
"So, crazy as this sounds, please listen to
a plan *mashugana* enough to get
the three of us admitted to the nuthouse.
Imagine praise and tributes from his fellows,
a sort of honor role of avian
presenters. This is daft I know but feels
appropriate."

"It's wacky," Nestor said,
"yet wonderful . . . with flare. Yes, it could work.
I have some reservations, but they'll keep.
We should revisit the entire scheme
once finished. Let's work and then I'd like to speak.
Odysseus, a penny for your thoughts?"

"It's very clever, really. The funeral
will be like nothing ever seen before.
And Nestor's reservations—I too will wait
and see, but tell us more of what you have
in store."

"The other birds would speak of him.
The three of us, Briseis, other friends
would lend our human voices in their stead."

"Odysseus is right, the plan's ingenious.
You'll need music too—and not a dirge—
but something solemn and uplifting . . . perhaps
'The Lark Ascending,' the Ralph Vaughn Williams piece."

"If it will set the mood, we can play it
as guests assemble. Thank you."

"Tell us what else?"

"I'm on thin ice," Achilles answered. "What
about the Stevens' poem, 'Thirteen Ways . . .'"

"'of Looking at a Blackbird,'" Odysseus
inserted. "That's terrific."
                              "More than that,
it's fitting," Nestor said.
                              "Thanks, I would do
a partial reading with judicious comments,
point out the parallels between the poem
and my relation with Patroclus. It's odd,
I don't know where all this is coming from,
perhaps a stirring of unconscious thoughts. . . ."
(Athena smiled, took no credit, but hoped
somehow Achilles would include the owl
and bridge her wisdom to the Stevens' poem).
        "Wait, let me get this straight. The idea is
to offer thirteen tributes in the mouths
of birds?" Odysseus was asking.
                              "Yes,
to recognize uniqueness by example.
Let's use the hoopoe from Farid Attir's
great Sufi epic, *The Conference of the Birds*."
        "You know that book? Amazing," Nestor said.
        "I don't know how I know it, but I do."
        "The rising phoenix is self-generating,"
Odysseus suggested. "It's a shoo-in."
        "It is," said Nestor. "Here's the counterpoise:
the sparrow and the ugly noose from *Cosmos*
by Gombrowicz is a must, I think."
        A pained expression crossed the Biker's face.
"The turtle dove should be a part. It suits
Briseis' deep affection—and mine as well."

They had a list of thirteen birds in minutes.
In fact they had to edit out some choices.
From raven, crow, and blackbird, they axed Poe

and then Ted Hughes. Others they combined—
the pelican and cormorant were grouped.
Outright, they cut the peacock and the duck.
     At last they divvied up the thirteen parts.
Besides themselves and, of course, Briseis,
they added Agamemnon, Menelaus,
Ajax Gross and Ajax Kurtz, Machaon,
Idomeneus, Meriones, and Thetis,
Eurybates. Wise Nestor added Thetis.
(Machaon and Eurybates! Go figure.)
     The Biker paused, for he had second thoughts.
"Why not retain the parts among us four?
Vaughn Williams is one, and with the other twelve,
we'll each have three. The service will cohere.
We'll take the weight. Our friends can mourn as called."

"So here's my view of the entire project."
As gently as he could, wise Nestor tried
to pry the Biker from the grip of madness.
"Achilles, listen to me, please. You feel
a loss that's real. It is. I'll grant you that.
But you've been overtaken by a demon.
Patroclus' grisly death impairs your judgment.
(Concealed, Athena listened and approved.)
Dear as he is to you, he is a bird.
A bird, Achilles, please consider that.
Your loss aside, extensive rites, I think,
are not appropriate. Your peers will judge
you harshly if the plan goes forward. I know
I am in part to blame by helping you,
but as I think about it now, we ought
to reconsider."
     Achilles bristled, stood,
and paced the room. "A comrade must be honored.

Even you, for all your wisdom, do
not understand the depth of love I have
for him. He was my brother. I always felt
his presence. Always. Only a bird? Hardly.
A spirit is more like it. I will not shirk
my duty, turn aside from what I owe
a friend, and bury Patroclus like a pet.
He was a force for life in me surpassing
every other love. I do not say
this lightly. Briseis, whom I love so deeply
you can't imagine, cannot replace Patroclus.
My friends, we will perform these rites as planned.
I cannot bear a less than perfect tribute."

Odysseus deferred to Nestor who
reached out to put Achilles' fears at ease:
"My friend, as far as I'm concerned, the plan
remains as is. Let's say no more of this.
I'll put the text in order, flesh it out,
and contact friends and guests. Odysseus,
I'd love your help with subtleties and color.
Achilles, I don't need to mention tasks.
Of course prepare the body of your friend,
arrange for music and set up the space.
And catering and flowers, sundry details."
        And so a concrete plan took form to hold
a celebration of Patroclus' life
in three days' time.

                        Achilles sat in thought.
He was in trouble technically. Who
imagined taxidermy to be among
the skills he needed? He went to Amazon
and bought an e-book and carefully began:

He placed Patroclus, Bird of Paradise,
face up and opened him along the line
that ran from pubis to the throat, reflected
skin, and cut the ribs with garden shears.
He pulled the organs from the body, as if
to follow Barron Rokitansky's method
(who, by the way, befriended Joseph Skoda,
the uncle of Emil, whose feats were chronicled
for you by Nestor in a lighter moment):
He took Patroclus' organs as a block,
set them in a plastic bag—to fire
after the hero's sacred rites were done—
and, then, without embalming, gently washed
the chest and belly cavities and stuffed
the space with paper towels. He closed the whole—
a running stitch was used—rewashed Patroclus
and plumped the feathers to cover the incision.
The Biker went to Office Depot, bought
some liquid paper, and restored Patroclus'
dingy feathers to their former whiteness.
Then next he used Briseis' black mascara
on beak and claws and nestled him among
fresh boughs of spruce. In anger he aligned
the wizened claw retrieved from Hector's belt
and covered the disunion with a sprig.

Patroclus lay in state beside the lectern.
A violin and keyboard greeted mourners
with haunting, joyous sounds that summoned life.
        Achilles spoke. "We chose 'The Lark Ascending'
as symbol of Patroclus' vaulted soul,
our hope that it will soar, find union with . . ."
he choked, not sure with what he wanted union.
He drew a breath, brushed back his tears, then sobbed.

Wise Nestor rose and rescued the occasion.
"Find union with the Mystery," he said
and flawlessly continued. "May grace and sweetness
seize his soul, may life infuse our friend.
To ask for life misphrases our request.
We don't know what we mean. We have no way
but metaphor to pray—that is the word—
to cosmic forces indifferent to petitions.
What god or gods are there to hear our pleas?
Yet we must ask. Our love demands we send
our hopes into a void that cannot care.
We pray it grants the union of his soul
with energies we cannot comprehend."
   And looking at Achilles who seemed in no
condition to resume, the sage went on,
"Tonight they're thirteen tributes to Patroclus
all befitting his uniqueness. His peers—
all avian—will speak for him through us.
You've heard the first, the freely soaring lark."
   Then Nestor offered his prepared remarks:
"Achilles asked that I speak next. We have
a need for closure of a heinous crime
so black, so ghastly the only word for it
is 'desecration.' Hector's deed was set
in motion by Apollo Fuente's wiles.
In Argentina, Fuente knew a Pole,
Witold Gombrowicz, whom Hitler's lightning blitz
left stranded there. He had no choice. He stayed.
His novel *Chaos* tells a grizzly tale:
A garroted bird, left hanging by death's wire,
was discovered dangling by two boys.
The Hammer's weapon and ensuing strife
derive from this example the meddler lifted
from Gombrowicz' book. He could have stopped
the degradation of Martillo honor,

but he did nothing to turn aside vendetta.
This is the source of Hector's wanton plan.
It shows how gods can make us suffer pain,
disgrace, humiliation, all for their pleasure.
Enough, for there are other tales to hear."

    A wave of anger coursed across the room,
and there was talk of arson. Nestor shushed
the restive partisans who sought revenge.

Briseis stood and gathered all attention.
"How much I feel the weight of unjust death
as if crude Hector smothered me and stoned
my corpse. Right now I must remember life,
the love Patroclus and Achilles shared,
their love for me as well. The turtle dove
has always meant devotion, and in this
our Bird excelled. His passion was so frenzied
that you could see the raptor rage in him
but always in defense of love or honor.
I cannot say he was monogamous—
we shared a love among the three of us.
He was attentive, generous, and kind.
He was a brother, lover, friend, and consort.
    "I now commend his noble soul to heaven
and to the phoenix, his eternal partner.
If there's rebirth of any sort, I ask
the phoenix to resurrect his buoyant soul,
for surely he deserves eternity.
There's more to say about the phoenix, but . . ."
she stopped to pull a tissue from her sleeve
and blew her nose. "I can't go on. I loved
that bird too much." And she began to weep.

Odysseus stood up and almost whispered,
"Briseis, words well-chosen. I'm sorry for

your loss. This Bird—this sentient Patroclus—
was a paradox. A hummingbird
amongst us all. The darting, brilliant mask—
all children love their colors and their flits
in flowered gardens. They evince composure—
a purpose with a guile so sharp they can
excise a heartbeat from an adversary
with their razor wings and never miss
a beat. Patroclus was a comrade in arms.
If I should ever undertake a journey—
and journeying is what I do—I'd ask
him first to come before recruiting others.
Who would want to lose this harrier?
We cannot know the future, but some things
like tides and moons are certain: this force in bright
attire, his tactics as a friend, his hallmark,
'Do it, do it,' are lost to us forever.
What raged for us, this rapier for the good,
has passed to other tasks. The Bird is dead."

Then Nestor rose again and stood out front.
"Our next is, what?, a quiet homily
about the avian questing soul,
a Sufi story by the brilliant poet,
Farid ud-Din Attar. This seer recounts
a conference of a thousand birds that flocked
to find the One. The hoopoe bird engages
their travails in distant lands to seek
the Simorgh, something we might call the face
of God. Most birds are lost, but thirty last.
I must correct the text we have. It's been
corrupted by a sage who claimed the parrot
fell from the flight toward immortality.
In truth at journey's end he was among
the thirty fellow travelers of the hoopoe.

They found what our Patroclus lived: a god
that guided from within. That's what he had,
a sense of god within his soul—and wrath
as righteous as Jehovah's. The hoopoe led
the birds to self-reflection but failed to see
that war and wisdom might collude to yield
a state of grace and hasten decent acts.
Our wise Patroclus understood that all
good works include god-sanctioned exercise
of power. The raptor lover of Achilles,
he wielded force and tenderness as one."

Moist-eyed Achilles, sad and shaken, stood,
"Thank you for taking over, Nestor. I guess
I lost it. My bent is practical. I didn't
know what to say, so thank you for the help,
and thank you for the parable as well.
       "I have a thousand thoughts about the bird
who shared my life, but I'll be brief tonight.
I'll speak of only one for just a moment,
and it concerns the mystery of union,
a trinity that Wallace Stevens raised
in "Thirteen Ways of Looking at a Blackbird,"
and honestly—I am an engineer—
I heard this poem by chance on NPR.
It talks about a man and woman's oneness
and says that blackbird, man, and woman are
a oneness too. Well, you can understand
that I was taken. I merged the three of us,
Patroclus—white macaw, of course, not black—
Briseis, and me, troika-like, to pull
the sled of our joint being. Nothing splits
this chaos-blocking unity . . ."
                              The squeal
of rusty hinges breached his eulogy.

Then through the gate Athena came disguised
as Henrietta Markham, wearing jeans,
and a Texan jersey stenciled "Xanthus."
(Sly goddess knew the value of *bon mots*.)
    "Hold it. I hate to blow the whistle, but
I have to reign in your charade, Achilles.
So pure and simple, you have parrot fever.
You need Olympic tetracycline now."
    "Just who the hell are you? Get out of here."
    "So here is language you can understand:
No way, I'll stick to you like dingleberries
to the butt end of a feral pig—
Achilles, someone has to ride your ass.
Besides, you know. I'm Henrietta Markham."
Then sotto voce to Achilles spoke
the goddess, "Don't pretend, that you don't know
that I'm Athena. Listen, I've got you by
your dendrites, pal, the short hairs of your neurons.
You needed help with Hector. Then, there was
no problem. Now, it seems amnesia grips you."
    Next Ajax Kurtz came forward with a leer—
the very same he flashed Cassandra at
the Jung Center. And then he licked his lips.
    "I don't intimidate. Ask Kyle LeFrac."
She pulled her father's ice pick from a sleeve.
    "Look, Henrietta, can we get this thing
on track? I want to bury my Patroclus."
    "We no can do, Achilles. It's dead as sin
is live. And by the way, you're overmatched.
My ice pick to your tire iron—no contest."
    The gray-eyed goddess brought Achilles to
his knees—and dressed as Henrietta Markham.
    At last he understood. Resigned, he looked
at her and said, "What would you have me do?"

"We'll shut this caper down right here, but first
you must give up your sidecar's sundry baggage:
the Bird, Briseis, Mestor's wife and Hector—
detritus life bestowed on you, the death
you rained on life—hyenas that stalk and sap
your psyche, beckon, and ensure its death."

Then Aphrodite touched Athena's thigh,
as if to settle scores for her disgrace
that madcap afternoon in her boutique.
She spat a stream of venom and complaints.
        The goddess was incensed at her intrusion,
"How dare you touch me, you lush hussy of
men's souls. I'm chaste. I hate the way that you
and Paris did a number on me, and so
I stopped his brother for Achilles' noose
and neutralized you in your barren ploy.
Your supplicants, these sordid men of yours,
deserve no more attention than the pigs
your lackey agent Circe made of them.
You swineherd, you are a wind-tossed mandala,
a sand painting in a torrid gale
of lust, a false imago of deceit.
Touch me again and I'll take you apart."
        That's how she chastened the goddess from Cythera.

"We should clean up this mess and call it quits,
move on," Athena said.
                        Achilles sputtered,
"The Hammer's corpse is in the freezer. What . . ."
        Defiantly Athena stood arms folded.
"I told you. Pull the plug, he stinks already."
        "The cast is union, and Actors' Equity
won't like your closing down their roles this early."

"You still don't get it. I'm in charge, Achilles.
They'll find work. Your lot has soldiered on
three thousand years. Don't worry."

"And Briseis,
my love beyond all else? I want her always
with me."

"Trust me, you don't. You only think
you do. Remember you abandoned her."

"I want her in, Athena."

"No, she's out,
Achilles, suck it up! I'll be the judge
of what is right for you. Get used to it."

"Do I have a choice?"

"Achilles, stop."

"And what about an *Iliad* for Houston?"

"You've murdered Mestor, Mestor's wife, and Hector
without remorse, abandoned Thetis and
Briseis. Our readers got their money's worth."

"What will become of my best friend Patroclus?"

"Achilles, please, let go of all of it."

"Not easy, he's a part of me, like you."

"Not true, Achilles, he's a bird. You conjured
a comrade in arms. A bird, a motley bird."

"And me, Athena, what will become of me?"

"I'm benching you. Beginning now, you'll sit
next season out."

"I want to play. I want
prime time—and honor, women, dominance—
a feature story on Fox or CNN."

"My friend, it's done for now. It is my way
or free agency. That's it. You choose.
This is the deal I offered many others:
I'll have control. You'll get the outward credit.
If not, you're on your own. Good luck adrift

in a wine-dark sea without a guide like me.
Take it. That's my advice. But you decide.
You want to spend eternity archived
in moldy tomes or live through me, Achilles?
With me, you'll live to fight another day.
Just trust me, it's nice work and you can get it."
    "My dear Patroclus who art in Heaven,"

                                        "Stop,

Achilles. Don't make it harder than it is.
Anima replacement therapy
is what you need to heal your subluxation.
We must reprogram every blessèd neuron
and superglue your psyche back together.
And you don't have a single guiding crone
of any sort. You need one for her wisdom.
I can't do all the heavy lifting. And what
about some shades of love not sullied by
the goddess from Cythera. I'll put out feelers
for Isolde, Heloise, and Ruth.
Let's set aside the gamy Greeks.
There's always too much downside risk with them.
We've got to get you off bewitching babes
and birds that rub your privates publicly.

    "Play ball, my friend. The parts I have in mind
for you Brad Pitt can't play. Now heel, Achilles,
your healing hinges on it, you dog-faced would-be
demigod. And if you don't, I'll teach
your sweet ass the meaning of 'Avenger.'

    "And so, Achilles, don't look back, my friend,
or I, your guide, will slip away from you—
Eurydice cast down and out of reach.
But tossed like plankton on the sea, absorb
the bioluminescence from within.
In time, look up and out with me. Right now,

the darkness poised below will swallow you.
One day we'll go together. Dante's plan
won't work in our chaotic times. You have
no elders, father, sage to shepherd you.
No Virgil. So a woman must extend
a hand as conduit and commissure
to lead you down on your tenebrous path,
then surge you toward a surer healing light.
     "Achilles, hope in vain that you're not cursed
to wander in and out of darkness. No man
escapes that fate. Your only balm is that
with luck from time to time your soul will prosper."

PRONUNCIATION OF PROPER NAMES

General readers will have no trouble with many names; Achilles and Aphrodite are in common use. But what about Briseis or Eurybates? To help I have provided a simplified phonetic pronunciation guide to these names. Modern speakers in the U.S. vary in how they pronounce classical Greek names; I have simply chosen one that feels right to me and works poetically: Odysseus, for example, is four syllables, not three. In the guide below, the major stress is in bold italics and the minor one(s) in plain italics. Common English language names (Swann, Lightman, etc.) are pronounced as we would in everyday speech.

Achilles (a-***kil***-eez)

Aeneas (ay-***nay***-uhs)

Agamemnon (*a*-ga-***mem***-non)

Agenor (a-***jee***-nor)

Ajax Gross (***ay***-jax)

Ajax Kurtz (***ay***-jax)

Aphrodite (*af*-ro-***deye***-tee)

Apollo (a-***pol***-loh)

Ares (***air***-eez)

Athena (a-***thee***-na)

Atrides (a-*tri*-des)

Briseis (bri-*say*-is)

Cassandra (kuh-*san*-druh)

Chryseis (kri-*say*-is)

Cythera (see-*ther*-ra)

Ekheklos (e-*keek*-los)

Euphorbus (yoo-*for*-bus)

Eurybates (yoo-*rib*-a-*teez*)

Fuente De La Luz (*fuen*-te *day* la *loose*)

Hector (*hek*-tur)

Helen (*hel*-en)

Idomeneus (eye-*do*-men-*yoos*)

Laerteson (lay-*air*-tes-*son*)

Leda (*lee*-da)

Machaon (ma-*kay*-on)

Martillo (mar-*tee*-yo)

Menelaus (*men*-uh-*lay*-uhs)

Mestor (*mes*-tor)

Meriones (mer-*ee*-on-*enz*)

Nestor (*nes*-tor)

Odysseus (oh-*dis*-ee-*uhs*)

Othryoneus (oh-*thre*-oh-*neus*)

Paris Alejandro (*par*-is *a*-lay-*han*-dro)

Patroclus (pa-*trok*-lus)

Peleuson (pe-*lay*-oo-*son*)

Pentha (*pen*-tha)

Phoenix (*fee*-niks)

Poseidon (po-*seye*-don)

Priam (*pri*-am)

Sapienza (*sap*-i-*en*-za)

Thetis (*thee*-tis)

ACKNOWLEDGMENTS

A special thanks to my wife Susan Abel Lieberman for her thoughtful comments, her wise good sense, her tolerance of my obsession to bring Homer to Houston, and her unfailing support.

I am grateful to Paul Ruffin for his faith in me as a poet. His unflagging commitment has been essential in bringing this project to fruition. Tom Baker, Carolyn Florek, Frank Krull, Sandi Stromberg, and Paul Woodruff as well as Susan Lieberman provided crucial feedback on the manuscript. They were gentle in pointing out my many errors and infelicities. It wasn't all sweetness and light, but thank you. Thanks also to Eden Elieff for excellent editorial help and to Kim Davis and Alec Brewster at Texas Review Press for their copy editing, layout, and design skills.

I am self-taught with respect to the classics and know no Greek, and so I am especially indebted to the work of the following scholars and writers for explication of *The Iliad*: Seth Benardete, Bernard Knox, Daniel Mendelsohn, Adam Nicolson, Jonathan Shay, and Paul Woodruff. Always in the background are the works of C.G. Jung, Joseph Campbell, and their contemporary proponents James Hollis and Ronald Schenk.

As for *The Iliad* itself, I have relied on the translations of Robert Fagles, Robert Fitzgerald, anAlexander Pope and to a lesser extent the work of William Cullen Bryant, George Chapman, Richmond Lattimore, and Christopher Logue.

An excerpt from Book I of *The Houstiliad* first appeared in *The Methodist DeBakey Cardiovascular Journal*.